What Did Their Future Hold?

As they flew over the impressive lodge, Mickie began to see a new side of Matt Greenslade. "You built that?" she asked, her voice a blend of amusement and admiration. "You certainly seem to like expensive toys."

"My investments aren't toys, Mickie. I quickly grow bored with games. If you haven't already, you'll learn soon enough that there's very little in life that I don't take dead seriously."

Mickie tensed in response. "You've described my own feelings exactly, Matthew Greenslade."

JUNE TREVOR

is a true world traveler who has visited or lived in more than twenty countries, including Spain, Italy and Mexico. She currently lives in California, where she devotes her time equally to her writing and her husband.

Dear Reader:

SILHOUETTE DESIRE is an exciting new line of contemporary romances from Silhouette Books. During the past year, many Silhouette readers have written in telling us what other types of stories they'd like to read from Silhouette, and we've kept these comments and suggestions in mind in developing SILHOUETTE DESIRE.

DESIREs feature all of the elements you like to see in a romance, plus a more sensual, provocative story. So if you want to experience all the excitement, passion and joy of falling in love, then SILHOUETTE DESIRE is for you.

I hope you enjoy this book and all the wonderful stories to come from SILHOUETTE DESIRE. I'd appreciate any thoughts you'd like to share with us on new SILHOUETTE DESIRE, and I invite you to write to us at the address below:

Karen Solem
Editor-in-Chief
Silhouette Books
P.O. Box 769
New York, N.Y. 10019

JUNE TREVOR
Winged Victory

Silhouette Desire
Published by Silhouette Books New York
America's Publisher of Contemporary Romance

Other Silhouette Books by June Trevor

Until the End of Time

 SILHOUETTE BOOKS, a Division of Simon & Schuster, Inc.
1230 Avenue of the Americas, New York, N.Y. 10020

Copyright © 1983 by June Trevor

Distributed by Pocket Books

ISBN: 0-671-47380-8

First Silhouette Books printing September, 1983

10 9 8 7 6 5 4 3 2 1

America's Publisher of Contemporary Romance

Printed in the U.S.A.

1

━━∞∞∞∞∞∞∞∞∞∞━━

Beyond the right wing tip of the Supercub the world was silver-blue and crystalline white. Mickie Kilpatrick dipped the wing of her powerful little plane so that she had a clearer view of the Bering Strait stretching in icy desolation from the Alaskan coastline to the northern edge of Russia, one hundred miles away. It was mid-April and the vast, frozen sea had begun its retreat from the shelf ice clinging to the rugged cliffs of Alaska's Seward Peninsula. Great ice packs floated offshore, their rough surfaces gleaming where the spring sun caught their knife-edged ridges.

Mickie had always looked forward to spring's approach which brought a breath of new life to the frozen North. Along with the kittiwake gulls and salmon returning to their Alaskan breeding grounds, the caribou herds would begin their mass migrations across the tundra in search of food. Not long afterward would come the sportsmen.

In the past it had been the hunters and fishermen who had kept Mickie's charter plane service alive. She had known that if she could make it through the long, frigid winter, with small bank loans to augment the meager weather station contracts and routine mail runs, her business would quickly be in the black again come summer. But that was the past.

A slight frown creased her brow above her gray eyes as she recalled yet again the circumstances that would confront her once she touched down on the airstrip in Nome. The Kilpatrick bush line would no longer be entirely her own. With the signing of her name to a contract the week before, Mickie had relinquished controlling interest to a buyer whom she had never met. The offer had been the only one she'd received and it had not been an ungenerous one, but for the fact that the buyer would not agree to a fifty-fifty arrangement. Through all the negotiations via mail and telephone with her agent, the buyer had been insistent on that point. Evidently he wanted no partner who might interfere with his plans: He demanded absolute control to run the line as he saw fit. The buyer—her new boss—would be there when she landed, waiting to check out the goods that his wealth had purchased.

Mickie's pride rankled at the idea that she would be someone else's employee. The line had been a family business from the beginning thirty-two years before when her father, Michael Kilpatrick, had begun his bush pilot career with a battered Stinson Gullwing. Mickie's mother had died when the girl was just three years old, so she had been raised by her father with the help of their sharp-tongued old housekeeper, Annie Obluk.

Long association with the native Alaskans had taught Kilpatrick the value of equality and mutual respect between the sexes. The Eskimos' survival in the frozen North had depended on the notion that each man and woman had tasks and that each was equally important. Mike Kilpatrick had seen the principle in action and had approved of it heartily, long before women's lib had become a chic byword. So he hadn't raised his daughter Mickie as if she'd been a fragile bundle of femininity. He had taught her to fly even before she could handle a jeep or snowmobile on the ground, and she'd obtained both her driver's license and pilot's credentials within weeks after she had turned sixteen.

That had been eight years earlier. After graduating from high school in Nome, Mickie had enrolled in a meteorology program at the University of Alaska in Anchorage. Her education had ended two years later with the sudden death of her father. Mickie had returned immediately to Nome where, despite her grief and initial regret at her interrupted schooling, she plunged into the business of running the Kilpatrick flying service single-handedly. It had been her father's life and she was determined that it would be hers as well.

Business had gone well the first two years. It had been so successful, in fact, that she'd made tentative plans to secure a bank loan to purchase another plane and expand the charter line. But the succeeding two winters had shattered that dream and she had been forced to obtain loans not for expansion but for daily survival. The first stroke of bad luck had been mechanical failure aloft, unforeseen and devastating. Mickie had survived the crash landing, but had spent thousands of dollars to repair the Cub. Her second stroke of ill fortune had involved a dreamy-eyed prospector who had left her with an unpaid $4,500 flying bill.

It had been a crushing financial blow. While her bankers had been sympathetic, they'd also been firm in stating that no additional loans would be forthcoming. If she was to avoid bankruptcy she would have to find a partner willing to absorb the losses of the preceding two years.

"Well, I've found a little more than I bargained for," Mickie told herself dryly as her practiced eyes restlessly surveyed the miles of flat terrain extending eastward beyond the Cub's left wing.

In the past she'd equated the vast immensity of the tundra with freedom, its uncluttered distances touched by little more than the cold winds blowing in off the ice-flecked sea. She'd even felt a certain sense of kinship with that solitude. Mickie had prided herself on her stubborn independence, much as her father had. The other pilots teased her about her attitude, but none had really ever tried to breach her prideful barrier except in a gruff, comradely fashion—which suited her just fine. Since she'd taken over the bush line she'd had neither the time nor the inclination for romantic involvement. Every man she met was held up to the measure of her father, perhaps even without her realizing it. Michael Kilpatrick had been cool, intelligent and utterly self-reliant, and had urged his daughter to be the same. "Be your own woman," he'd told her over and over again from the time she was ten years old. "Don't depend on any man."

Now look what I've done, she thought, the cool gray eyes that were so like her father's threatening to brim over with tears. I've practically sold my birthright to a stranger.

Mickie shook her head as if to deny the glistening wetness beginning to cloud her vision. As she did so a mass of coppery curls slipped forward over the fur-trimmed edge of her parka hood. Despite the fact that she kept her hair fairly short, the curls were unruly at any length and gave her a tousled, gaminlike appearance. But the innocent look was deceiving: The tiny lines beyond the corners of her lovely eyes bespoke experience and a hint of tiredness. And more often than not, in recent months, her generous mouth was apt to be undercut by a subtle hardness of expression. Mickie was a woman, a woman fighting for her existence in the only world she had ever known. How would her new "employer" fit into her life as it had been up until this point?

For the hundredth time that week she wondered what the man would be like. She knew nothing at all about him except his name: Matthew Greenslade. Perhaps, she thought hopefully, he wanted nothing more than a tax write-off and would be content to let her see to the day-to-day operation of the flight business. But the hope died almost as quickly as it had arisen. An astute businessman would not have to travel to the Arctic outreaches in order to find a useful tax shelter. Her instincts told her that only a man deeply interested in flying and in the rugged land itself would choose to burden himself with a financially shaky bush service.

Mickie tossed her head in a prideful gesture. Her business losses were the result of ill luck rather than poor management. She had nothing to be ashamed of. Still, her eyes darkened momentarily with a flicker of despair as they roved to the distant horizon. Mickie felt that she was backed into a corner . . . yet, perversely, she didn't give up hope that somehow she might fight her way out.

A few minutes later her thoughts were concentrated totally on the business of flying as Nome came into view in the distance, a brave outpost of civilization at the edge of the vast tundra. The town lay south of the Arctic Circle and had a little under ten thousand inhabitants, considerably lower than the population high of twenty thousand it had boasted during the gold rush heyday in 1901. One of the pioneers who had remained in Nome was Mickie's grandfather, Dwight Kilpatrick, who had exchanged his mining tools for those of a trapper.

Mickie eased up on the throttle and nosed the plane gently downward until she skimmed several hundred feet above the rooftops of the treeless city. Streamers of curling smoke from a hundred chimneys informed her that there was an offshore breeze and she guided her craft out over icy blue Norton Sound before banking for a final approach to the airport runway. With one gloved hand she reached out to flick a switch, while with the other she picked up her radio. "This is C-one-three-four-five requesting okay to land," she said crisply.

"Come on in, C-one-three-four-five." The words

crackled over the transmitter. "Hi ya, Mickie. Welcome home." The voice was that of Sam Lansing, manager of the small but busy Nome airport.

Normally she would have smiled at hearing Sam's familiar greeting and made a bantering remark in return before touching down. But even as the snowy strip leaped up to meet the skis on her Cub her thoughts were rushing ahead to the dreaded meeting with Matthew Greenslade.

After cutting the engine Mickie opened the door and slid to the ground. The hard-packed snow crunched beneath her boots as she circled the plane, checking the condition of the skis and wing surfaces. Such caution and care had become second nature to her, since she knew that the Cub's performance depended on the exacting maintenance it received. But this time she performed her routine check with somewhat less enthusiasm than usual.

Knowing that she could no longer put off the inevitable, Mickie hurried over the snow toward the huddle of concrete buildings at the edge of the runway. Once inside she shrugged out of her jacket and ran nervous fingers through her curls, their coppery sheen a lively contrast to her gold earrings.

Despite her air of efficiency and superficial hardness, Mickie's femininity came as naturally to her as breathing. The sweater tucked into her jeans delineated her lithe figure to perfection. She stopped for an instant before a mirror in the hallway and smoothed down the soft wool, its wintry-heather weave picked up in the gray and mauve of the scarf knotted at her throat.

Then Mickie walked on, her boots tapping swiftly as she passed the row of open office doors and waved distractedly to the secretaries inside. Her thoughts were centered on the difficult encounter ahead of her. Finally she stopped before a door with its unobtrusive name-plate, KILPATRICK, and took a deep breath before walking inside.

To her surprise she found the small outer office empty. There was no business tycoon waiting impatiently for her arrival. There was nothing but the old typewriter and desk where her father's secretary Jean Burns had worked before she'd quit five years earlier and moved to Fairbanks. Mickie smiled a little as she glanced at the secretary's nameplate, still affixed to the desk's front edge. Underlying the nostalgic smile, however, was a slight but unmistakable feeling of relief. Evidently Matthew Greenslade hadn't yet arrived, and, for the time being at least, life was as it had always been. She hung her coat on its hook and picked up the stack of mail from the table, idly glancing through it as she pushed open the door leading to her private office.

Glancing up she was stunned to find herself staring at a pair of boots, casually crossed and planted squarely on the middle of her desk. Beyond the boot tips she glimpsed a shock of thick, black hair. After the briefest moment of stunned silence she strode forward and tossed the mail down before the dark leather soles. "What do you think you're doing?"

With unimaginable swiftness the boots swung down from the desk top and their owner sat facing her directly, whiskey-colored eyes ablaze with impatience. "Where the devil have you been, Miss Burns?" He cut through her angry query with a deep, annoyed voice. "I don't see how Kilpatrick can expect to run an efficient operation when his secretary is away from her desk for hours at a time."

Mickie crossed her arms and stared down at the man, her gray eyes darkening like storm clouds. "The Kilpatrick line hasn't had a secretary for years, Mr. . . . Greenslade, I assume," she replied with a wry, deceptively quiet air.

"That's right. I'm Matt Greenslade. Now, are you going to keep me in suspense while I'm forced to guess who the hell you are?" He pushed himself away from the desk and stood up, the width of his shoulders beneath the suede aviator's jacket projecting solid strength.

She paused for a long moment, allowing her eyes to survey him coolly: the black hair streaked lightly with silver, the high-bridged nose and lean face that gave him a hawklike air. "Okay, no more suspense," she said at last, feeling his gaze harden at the deliberately provoking slowness of her reply. "I'm Mickie Kilpatrick."

Greenslade relaxed. "Ah, I see. The owner's daughter," he replied with a casual, dismissive air as his hands moved to make neat stacks of the folders and papers that he'd been leafing through. "When can I expect Kilpatrick?"

"Your second wrong assumption of the day, Mr. Greenslade." She couldn't quite keep the contempt out of her voice, nor the pride, as she added, "I'm the only Kilpatrick you'll have to deal with. The flying service is mine."

A mingled look of disbelief and curiosity flashed in his eyes as he sat down once again. He turned away from her in the chair, his head thrown slightly back as he regarded the wall-sized topographical map of northwestern Alaska before him. When he swiveled round again Mickie caught the look of subtle amusement in his gaze. "Your business agent never once told me I was dealing with a woman," he replied, the rough timbre of his voice smoothed by an undercurrent of laughter. "It was always 'Kilpatrick wants this' or 'Kilpatrick demands that,' and I figured the tough old pilot was out to make the best deal for himself. I flew out with him on a hunting charter six years ago and I was impressed by the guy. Where is he now?"

Nettled by his attitude of amused and faintly condescending surprise, she regarded him stonily. "My father died four years ago of a heart attack. I run the line now." Mickie bit her lip as the words echoed in her own mind. She no longer ran anything at all: The past was a closed chapter and the future sat before her, a pair of mocking eyes and dark, calloused hands. Then Mickie spoke again, almost arrogantly, as if her pride could battle his derisive humor. "Believe me, I would have continued to run the service, too, if I hadn't been plagued by bad luck the past two winters."

"Is that what you call it?" he asked with rough impatience, no trace of amusement left. "I'd say it was bad judgment . . . pure and simple."

The anger which had been simmering beneath the surface of Mickie's deceptively calm gray eyes threatened to erupt. "I suppose you're referring to the Johnstone matter. You've had plenty of time to read the details of the matter since making yourself at home in *my* office with *my* private papers," Mickie retorted, her voice brittle with sarcasm.

Greenslade stood up. "I'm going to remind you of something once and once only. You relinquished your right to a 'private' office and 'private' papers having to do with this business the instant you signed your name to that contract last week. You know the terms of the agreement as well as I."

But Mickie would not be deflected from the speech of self-defense that she'd begun. "Any pilot would have jumped at the Johnstone contract when he breezed into Nome with his Arctic research plans. How could I or anyone else have known he'd turn out to be a penniless fraud?"

"You might have relied a little less on trust and a little more on advance money," he countered dryly. Then, as if the current discussion were little more than boring past history, he turned again to the huge map. "Would you mind explaining the blue and yellow pins that you've set in the map?"

With slow reluctance she moved to join him on the other side of the desk. For the moment, at least, her anger was spent. Time and again since Johnstone had left her with his worthless check Mickie had berated herself for not doing precisely what Greenslade had pointed out. If she had demanded advance money from the deluded prospector, perhaps she wouldn't have found herself in this humiliating position with Matthew Greenslade now. As she came to stand beside him Mickie felt his impatient eyes on her.

He sat down on the edge of the desk. "Well, Kilpatrick? Am I going to have to fight you every step of the way?"

She drew a ragged breath, quelling her anger until there was no visible sign of it but for two high spots of color on her cheeks. "The blue pins represent my regular runs, mail and supply drops and so forth." She gestured with her head, her hands still folded defensively before her. "The yellow pins are special charters—one-time flights to ferry sportsmen out into the back country."

Though his eyes were still undeniably laughing when she turned to face him, she sensed a new interest.

"You do all the flying yourself?"

"Of course," she replied simply. "I have no choice."

His gaze seemed to measure her in some incalculable way. "Just how good a pilot are you, Kilpatrick Junior?"

Mickie ignored the gibe as she raised her chin in haughty defiance. "I was trained by the best, Mr. Greenslade."

He grinned, white teeth flashing against the hard mahogany of his features. "Call me Matt."

Mickie's eyes were like a frozen tundra pond. "I prefer not to."

He gave an indifferent shrug before turning once again to the huge map with its heavily pinpricked surface. "I can tell you straight out that the first change I'll probably make is to cut down on some of these outlying routes. I want to tighten up as much as possible." He stood up, indicating areas with one outstretched arm. "These island stops like Russian Harbor and the inland mountain villages should probably be dropped. I doubt if they generate much profit."

Mickie's eyes widened angrily. "How can you even consider such a move? My flights are essential to those isolated villages that you're prepared to write off so casually." She gave an energetic tug to the ends of her scarf before moving to stand between the map and Matt Greenslade, as if her physical presence could somehow prevent the curtailing of the flights. She placed her hands on her hips and gazed up at him defiantly, eyes sharp-edged as slate. "Isn't there such a word as compassion in your vocabulary?"

Greenslade perched on the edge of the desk, saying nothing in reply. His own eyes flicked downward from her full lips to the tantalizing outline of her breasts in the sweater; they seemed to register nascent approval, too, of the way her jeans conformed to the curving lines of her hips and thighs.

For the first time since they'd met that afternoon Mickie sensed that he was seeing her as a woman rather than an argumentative business associate. The realization sent tiny shock waves pulsating through her nervous system, forcing her, as it did, to recognize his lean and rough-cut masculinity. Staring back at his lazy, amber-eyed grin, Mickie was compelled to admit that some women might find a certain perverse and tigerish charm in him. But almost as swiftly as the thought had risen in her mind she quelled it. She knew that to admit to any such attraction would be to weaken her defiance against him. Mickie intended to fight him, with any and every weapon she could find, in order to keep her bush routes intact.

She resumed her animated attack. "If you can't fathom the meaning of compassion, then surely you can understand the harsh facts of survival. Besides, you can't possibly have bought into a bush line with the thought of realizing tremendous profits on your investment."

"You're right about that, at least, Mickie," he shot

back. "How can I hope to make a profit straight off when I have to begin by spending fifteen thousand dollars to pay off your outstanding debts?" Both his eyes and his tone mocked her. "But I didn't buy in to be a humanitarian, either. It happened to work in well with certain other business interests I have in the area."

"But it isn't fair for you to cut vital services to Russian Harbor and Ugashik," she argued stubbornly.

His topaz eyes bored into her. *"Life* isn't fair, Mickie. You might as well come to terms with that right now." Then he added roughly, "I hope you'll remember a couple of things. The first is that I bailed you and your sinking flight service out of trouble. I'm not fool enough to expect gratitude, but I do expect a little cooperation. The second thing is that under the terms of the agreement you work for me and not vice versa." He paused a moment before adding with slow deliberateness, "That means when I say jump, you jump, Mickie." There was the merest hint of a threat in his hard gaze.

Mickie tossed her head angrily. "And if I don't?" she whispered in defiance, reaching across the desk to retrieve a typed flight schedule.

As she did so his hand shot out and imprisoned hers roughly. "Then we'll have to work it out between us . . . one way or another." He released her hand as swiftly as he'd taken it and once more she saw the glint of challenge in his eyes.

2

The sharp confrontation between Mickie and Matt Greenslade ended when he strode out of her office, tossing a curt "Meet me at the plane" over his shoulder. She had dawdled purposefully for twenty minutes, neatly chalking her week's schedule on the board before refiling the papers and folders that he had helped himself to while awaiting her arrival.

When she finally slipped into her parka and stepped outside Mickie noticed without surprise that the sun was well past midpoint in its low arc above the horizon. At three-thirty the elongated shadows of evening were already stretching before her on the packed snow of the runway as she headed toward the Cub.

Matt Greenslade stood motionless on the far side of the plane, apparently indifferent to the bitter cold which deepened as the long, northern twilight approached. Mickie caught a glimpse of his profile as she walked around the Cub's tail and in that moment his features seemed made of granite. So immersed was he in his own thoughts, eyes fixed on some hazy point beyond the empty horizon, that he didn't stir until Mickie came to stand in front of him.

"Well, shall we be on our way? It's getting late," she

said impatiently, her tone as brittle as the frigid air. She
resented the aura of quiet solitude which he had drawn
about himself, and she found herself growing unreason-
ably annoyed that he had made no comment on her
defiant tardiness.

With lazy grace he straightened up from where he'd
been leaning against the right wing. His hands were
thrust into the pockets of his cords as he turned toward
his impatient companion. "The Cub looks better than I'd
imagined it would. There's hardly a trace of the hard
belly landing she took." He gestured with his chin toward
the plane's undercarriage.

Mickie glanced sharply at him, wondering if that
remark too somehow implied a criticism of her flying
judgment, but his eyes seemed to mirror nothing more
than grudging admiration for the sturdy, well-cared-for
plane. She relaxed then, although her brow was still
creased with vexation. "I was lucky," she conceded at
last. "Most of the damage was superficial."

"Let's get the Cub aloft. I'm curious to see exactly
what she's capable of and you seem anxious to show
me." The subtle outline of a grin played about his lips as
he yanked open the door. Gone was the granite stillness
that had annoyed her so inexplicably a moment earlier.
Matthew Greenslade was a hard-driving businessman
once again.

Mickie was taken aback by this abrupt shift in mood,
not knowing quite what to make of it. She sighed in
frustration, liking less and less the idea of a forced
business liaison with the hardheaded, unreadable stranger before her.

Then her thoughts were swallowed up by the familiar
whining roar of a snowmobile as the vehicle skidded
across the airstrip toward them. It halted next to the
Supercub and the airport operations chief hailed them.
After greeting Mickie, he turned to her companion.
"You're Matt Greenslade, aren't you? Sam said you'd

introduced yourself this morning. We're always glad to welcome another flyer to Nome. By the way, I'm Jim Iniak." He grinned as he jumped out of the snowmobile and reached across to shake hands.

"Thanks. It's good to be here. The one thing that's kept me coming north again and again is the friendliness and hospitality of you Alaskans." He shifted his gaze toward Mickie, eyes boring into hers with subtle irony.

"Glad to hear it!" Jim answered with a grin. "Listen, the reason I tore out here is to ask if you two can alter your flight plan a bit to drop these air express parcels in Kotzebue before you head out for Point Hope. They arrived today from Fairbanks and the gas workers up near the Pole are pretty anxious to get these parts. Once they get to Kotzebue there's a pilot available there to fly them on up to Barrow."

Mickie had remained by the Cub's open door as the two men had exchanged their friendly introductions, but when Jim made his request she immediately stepped forward. Before she could say a word, however, Greenslade had spoken for them both with cool assurance. "Sure thing. Throw them in the back." He took the bills of lading and glanced over them before thrusting them into the pocket of his jacket.

Anger smoldered in Mickie's eyes at having her authority so casually usurped by Greenslade. In that moment she might have walked away from the Cub and its arrogant new owner, preferring to sell out completely rather than be subordinate to him. But while Michael Kilpatrick had insisted that his daughter never become dependent on any man, he had at the same time instilled a strong sense of self-discipline. He would have disapproved even more of her running away from any situation—however unpleasant. Swallowing both her pride and her anger, Mickie climbed into the cockpit and cranked the engine.

A minute later Greenslade climbed in beside her.

"Let's go, Kilpatrick. Jim warned me that you're a tough cookie, but one of the best damned pilots around." He grinned over at her. "I want to see how much he exaggerated."

Mickie bit her lip to repress the sharp retort that bubbled to her lips, resolving not to let him discover how much his needling riled her. They taxied down the runway, then waited for clearance from the tower. Finally, Sam Lansing's voice crackled over the radio. "Go ahead, C-one-three-four-five. Bon voyage on your maiden flight, Mickie and Matt. Say, you two should rename the line the Double M! It's kinda catchy. Over." She glared at the radio as it transmitted his chortled advice, feeling oddly betrayed by the man who'd been a close friend of her father's for twenty years and who seemed to take this new change of affairs in the Kilpatrick line with such maddeningly cheerful bonhomie.

When Matt saw that his flying companion was making no effort to answer the tower he reached over and picked up the transmitter. "Thanks, Sam. We'll keep it in mind. Over."

The airport manager was all business when next he spoke. "Weather report's just come in. Strong storm front is brewing out over the Arctic Sea. Keep an eye on it. Over and out."

Mickie released the throttle fully and the Cub was soon airborne. They circled the field once, catching a glimpse far below of Jim Iniak and his snowmobile moving over the runway like a child's toy over white carpet. Then they were northward bound with no other companions than the vast, darkening sky and the ice-choked sea below them to their left.

Watching Greenslade curiously out of the corner of her eye, Mickie saw that he appeared to be taking compass readings. Several minutes later her unspoken curiosity was partially satisfied as her companion issued a crisp order. "Change heading now. I want you to set a course for seventy-five degrees northwest."

She turned to regard him directly, but his eyes were hidden behind dark aviator's glasses so that she could not discern their expression. "It's a little late in the day for sightseeing and there's bad weather approaching," she countered.

"This isn't an idle side trip. I told you earlier that I had other business interests in the area. One of the things that attracted me to your flight line was its strategic location in terms of my needs. I want to check out exact distances and flying times. Now," he added impatiently, "are you going to change course or do I have to order you out of the cockpit and fly this plane myself?"

She gritted her teeth in silent anger at his high-handed order, but nonetheless did as he directed. An hour passed and once more she felt curiosity overcoming her festering anger. "Where exactly are we headed? By the compass readings you gave me it sounds as though we're heading for the western foothills of the Brooks Range."

"It's reassuring to find out that my pilot knows her Alaskan geography so well. We're making for a point east of Eelek. Do you know the village?"

"Yes, my housekeeper Annie has relatives there," Mickie replied at once. "But the only other outpost east of it that I can think of is a tumbledown shack belonging to an old trapper called Harry LaCrosse. My Dad and I stopped there once on a cross-country dogsled race many years ago."

He grinned unexpectedly at that. "What else can you do, Kilpatrick? If I'd had any idea that I'd be dealing with a superwoman I might have had second thoughts about buying into the line," he teased.

Mickie felt herself laughing at his remark. "Maybe we both got more than we bargained for, Matthew Greenslade."

His lips twisted wryly. "I suppose you're a damn good shot with a hunter's rifle as well."

For the first time that day she was almost enjoying herself. The melodious laughter that had bubbled to her lips was reflected in her eyes, agleam like gray satin as she turned to regard the man beside her. "If I've set my sights on something, I don't often miss."

His response was low and barely audible over the steady throb of the plane's engine. "I'll remember that."

Mickie thought she heard an undercurrent of rough laughter as well, but the sound was swallowed up in the engine's drone. Directly ahead of them rose the Brooks Range, stretching away in miles of jagged, white peaks. The mountains were the northerly border of the great Alaskan central plateau, itself rising upward through forests of spruce and birch to the base of the ice-clad mountains.

She put the Cub on a southeasterly course and after thirty minutes Spruce Lake came into view, its far shore sloping in a wide natural amphitheater whose sides rose in sheer cliffs. As they approached more closely Mickie was astonished to see that Harry LaCrosse's weather-beaten shack had been replaced by a modern lodge. A rooftop terrace was enclosed by a Plexiglas dome, its triangular panes winking like pinpoints of fire in the last red glow of sunset.

"You built that, Greenslade?" she asked, her voice a blend of amusement and admiration. "You certainly seem to have a liking for expensive toys."

Glancing over at him, Mickie saw that he'd removed his sunglasses and his tawny eyes now seemed to catch the sun's dying glow. "My investments aren't toys, Mickie, and I quickly grow bored with games. If you haven't done so already, you'll learn soon enough that there's very little in life that I don't take dead seriously."

Mickie had banked the plane in a smooth, wide turn over the dark lodge and headed it on a northwesterly course towards Kotzebue. Now her hands tightened on the controls in response to his remark. "You've described my own feelings precisely, Matthew Greenslade."

He made no reply to that. Night deepened gradually around the plane until they seemed surrounded by a world of cold silence broken only by the reassuring monotonous throb of the engines. After a while Mickie spoke again. "I suppose the old LaCrosse site won't be a private retreat for you, then?" she asked, genuinely curious.

He shifted in the passenger seat, as if pulling himself back to the present from some distant reverie. "No. I built it as an all-season resort lodge. I liked the idea of creating an oasis of luxury in the middle of the Alaskan wilderness. Everything from the hot tub to the skylights was airlifted piece by piece from Anchorage."

"That's crazy!" Mickie replied spiritedly. "People want either luxurious surroundings or untamed country. They don't want both in the same place."

"You're wrong," he argued in a flat, almost bored monotone. "People crave novelty. They want what they think they can't have."

"Is that what motivates you?" Mickie asked quietly, emboldened by the impersonal black veil of night that seemed to invite confidences.

"I was describing other people's dreams, not my own. The only dream that motivates me is challenge. I'd rather bet on a thousand-to-one long shot any day than on a sure thing. That's why ten years ago I put my last five thousand dollars in an abandoned chromite mine and why I bought the LaCrosse site." He paused a moment before continuing. "That's why I bought your failing bush line, too, even before I knew there'd be the added spice of having to deal with an impossibly stubborn woman. Make no mistake about it," he added provokingly, the words deepened in the rarefied air of the tiny cockpit. "You've become part of the challenge."

"Every man has to confront failure sooner or later," she retorted, not wishing to admit even to herself that his half-teasing words had touched a sensitive nerve within her.

He grinned briefly at that. "I'm willing to take the risk."

The rest of the trip was completed in silence, both of them wrapped in their own thoughts. Mickie concentrated on flying once more. As they drew closer to the Arctic coast, streamers of racing fog swirled around the Cub. She brought the plane down a few hundred feet, hoping to avoid the blinding white mist, but the fog continued to surround them.

A short time later Mickie breathed a sigh of relief as she glimpsed the row of winking lights that were strung out like a gem-studded belt along the length of the one-street town. They touched down on the bleak airstrip beneath a lowering circle of scud that had closed around them within a matter of minutes. There was no question of continuing on that night to Point Hope. For better or worse, they were stuck in Kotzebue until morning at least.

After unloading the cargo destined for Barrow they hitched a ride into town in the airport Jeep. Mickie rarely flew into Kotzebue, preferring to take her flying service to the even more remote communities ringing the northwestern coast.

Because it was on a direct flight path from Nome the village was not as isolated as it appeared on the map; it was an outpost perched on the tip of a long finger of land just inside the Arctic Circle. Kotzebue had long been a traditional meeting point for Eskimo clans, but the village had expanded its role to become a modern hub for trappers, guides, bush pilots and tourists.

Wedged between Matt and the driver in the front seat of the vehicle, Mickie stared out beyond the fog to the shops and concrete-block buildings lining the graveled main street. Every window was dark, every door shut tight and padlocked. The ghost town aura lifted suddenly, however, as they turned a corner and golden light spilled into the darkness and fog from a large two-story building.

"I suspected you'd be wanting to hit Lil's place first thing." The driver grinned at his two passengers. "Hers is the only one open throughout the winter."

A battered sign advertising the Little Arctic Tavern creaked above the entryway. Staring up at it through the freezing mist, Mickie was reminded of the flights she'd made to Kotzebue with her father. Each trip would invariably end with a stop at Lil Chandler's tavern. Though she'd been a child at the time, Mickie could well remember that Lil had had a long-standing crush on her father, though the taciturn widower had never acknowledged the woman's admiration.

Matt Greenslade came up behind Mickie, who stood regarding the tavern sign with a bemused expression, and placed one hand lightly on her back while with the other he pushed open the wooden door before them. A blast of warm, smoky air, music and boisterous conversation greeted the pair as they stepped inside. Blonde, ample-bosomed and seemingly unchanged since Mickie had last seen her, Lil stood behind the bar, drying glasses with the edge of her muslin apron.

"Well, I'll be darned!" the tavern keeper cried with a smile of delight. "If it isn't Mike Kilpatrick's girl! I haven't seen you in years." Lil glanced past Mickie's shoulder. "And this must be your new flying partner. Greenslade, isn't it?" She extended a plump red hand across the bar to him.

Mickie was marveling to herself at the speed with which news traveled from one Arctic outpost to another when Lil spoke again, this time calling to a group gathered around one of the long plank tables that edged the dance floor. "Jake, Mickie Kilpatrick and her new partner have flown in." She urged Matt to join the group, but held Mickie back a moment. "Listen, sweetie," Lil advised in a motherly fashion, "the guys'll bunk out wherever they can tonight as long as this fog lasts, and anyway, they'll probably be up all hours playing poker. Just let me know when you're ready to turn in and I'll let you have my daughter Sally's room upstairs. She's gone to Anchorage for a few weeks and won't mind at all."

Mickie flashed the woman a grateful smile, then made her way to the crowded table. Jake Waller, a gregarious hunting guide and pilot, had already introduced Matt to everyone by the time Mickie joined them. Catching sight of her then, Jake came forward and tossed an affectionate arm around her shoulder. "It's good to see you again, kid. You've been a stranger around town since Mike died." His sharp blue eyes crinkled as he took in the lines of exhaustion about her mouth and eyes. "Bet you've been working like a fool, just like your old man used to do. If I ain't mistaken you've inherited his feisty independence, too." Jake shook his gray head. Further remonstrances were cut off as they arrived at the table and Jake reached down to lift his half-empty beer mug. "I was going to offer a toast to the new partnership, but I think we should pour a new round first. What'll you have, Mickie? Are you a teetotaler like Mike was? I never saw anyone put away so many quarts of milk at a sitting!"

"I didn't inherit all of Dad's traits." She grinned in return. "Actually, I wouldn't mind a cup of hot coffee laced with brandy. We had a long, cold flight in from Spruce Lake."

"Spruce Lake?" Jake turned to Greenslade. "Is that your place? I've been hearing stories about some fancy construction going on out there."

"That's right," Matt replied easily.

"Well, I suppose everyone's entitled to his crazy dreams." Jake grinned. The round of drinks had arrived, prompting the guide to lift his brimming mug. "Here's to Kilpatrick and Greenslade. May their line prosper!"

High-spirited laughter greeted this gruff testimonial

that somehow seemed more appropriate to a wedding feast than a friendly send-off to a new business partnership. Mickie drank the sweet hot coffee, grateful for the warmth which gradually infused her half-frozen limbs. Then someone else ordered another round and she found herself sipping hot grog swirled with melted butter. The potent rum-and-whiskey concoction was much too strong for her, but Mickie continued to sip at it, enjoying the sensation of warm lassitude that seemed to creep over her.

Then Harry Norton, another of Mike Kilpatrick's contemporaries, stood up to add his share to the merriment. Mickie's pretty laughter rang out over the baritone guffaws when the gray-haired pilot observed with mock solemnity, "I sincerely hope their union is a fruitful one."

Thoroughly immersed in the hilarious sham wedding feast which her father's buddies had embarked upon spontaneously, the "bride" herself at last stood up, swaying slightly as she held out her glass mug in Matt Greenslade's direction. The subtlest glimmer of malice rose in Mickie's clear eyes as she regarded him a moment before speaking. "To the *cheechako* who thought he could," she began, her soft voice rising above the low, expectant laughter that greeted her words. The Indian term was a half-disdainful, half-teasing reference to the naive newcomers to the state, who so brashly expected to tame and conquer overnight what longtime residents knew could not be brought within a man's scope in a full lifetime. After the muffled laughter had died down Mickie spoke again. "Alaskan mountains are like Alaskan women: beautiful but unconquerable. Many men have tried, but few have succeeded."

Matt's eyes shot sparks of fire as his gaze locked with hers above the heads of the old-timers around the table. Mickie stared back at him defiantly, her lips curved upward in a spiteful smile.

The taut moment of confrontation was broken as Jake

clapped Matt on the back, wiping away tears of mirth from his eyes with his other hand. "What a firebrand you've bound yourself to!" he cried. "Just be thankful she's your business partner and not your wife. Kilpatrick's kid won't buckle down to anybody! Say, would you mind if I was the first to give her a little spin around the dance floor?" he added, unwilling to end the vastly amusing marriage charade.

"Be my guest," Matt replied with deceptively lazy good humor. "Mickie's got quite a well-rounded speaking ability. I'll be curious to see how the rest of her measures up . . . so to speak."

Mickie caught the tail end of his words as Jake pulled her toward the crowded dance floor, but she chose to ignore them in favor of savoring the triumphant afterglow of the clever little speech she'd made at his expense.

The versatile combo had switched from country music to a lively set of big band melodies, so the gleeful hunting guide had the opportunity to lead his partner through a series of deftly executed jitterbug steps. A smattering of appreciative applause greeted their performance as the musicians made a smooth transition into a slower foxtrot rhythm.

"You're one hell of a dancer, Mickie," Jake said between gasps. "If I were twenty years younger I might make a play for you myself."

"You sly old fox!" she broke in laughingly. "I bet you've made plays for women from the time you were old enough to strut, but I bet that darned few of them have even come close to trapping you in their snares."

The grizzled old hunter chuckled. "Listen, kid. What's right for the gander ain't necessarily right for a sweet little goose like you."

"Jake," Mickie retorted with a teasing sigh as they moved toward the table, "you're hopelessly chauvinistic . . . but I like you anyway."

They were so engrossed in their joking repartee that they hadn't noticed Matt Greenslade's approach until he had stopped before them, an ironic grin on his lips. "The first dance was yours, Jake, but the second one's all mine," he remarked coolly, at the same time slipping an infuriatingly proprietary hand around Mickie's waist.

As soon as Jake had wandered back to his chair she tried to wriggle out of Matt's grasp. "I have no intention of dancing with you, Greenslade," she said, her eyes darkening with anger.

"You have no choice, do you, Mickie?" He grinned. "Unless you want to create a scene."

Recognizing the truth in that, she ceased her futile wriggling at once. He slipped both hands around her waist then, resting them in the soft curve above the swell of her hips. Mickie had no choice but to raise her elbows and rest them in the crook of his encircling arms. Through the rough wool of his shirt she became acutely aware of his tightly corded bicep muscles where her hands rested on them. They were more the arms of a man who wielded a sledgehammer for a living than those of some paper-pushing executive in his skyscraper office.

For the first time she found herself speculating curiously on his background. Where had his wealth come from? She remembered his casual mention of a chromite mine during their flight in. Even as her thoughts flitted from one possibility to another her hands began an unconscious exploration of the sinews and ligaments of his powerful upper arms.

"For such a sharp-tongued woman you have a surprisingly sensual touch," he murmured, a faint wisp of laughter catching on the rough edge of his voice.

Her eyes flew upward in perplexed alarm until she became aware of the intimate traceries which her fingers had been drawing of their own accord across his wool-clad skin. Mickie balled her traitorous hands into fists, grateful that the dim lighting hid the rising color in her cheeks. "What kind of dancing is this, anyway?" she complained, as a cover for her own confusion.

"Would you rather I held you closer?" Matt asked innocently.

Her eyelashes fluttered with telltale alarm while her back stiffened beneath the splayed fingers that held her like a spring-release trap, ready to snap shut if she attempted to escape.

"No!"

He laughed openly, eyes narrowed to amber slits. "Are you afraid of me, Mickie?"

"Certainly not!" she retorted hotly.

"Then maybe you should be. I already told you once today that I'm not a man to be trifled with."

Before she could reply the music drifted into a slower rhythm and he did precisely what he had threatened to do a moment earlier. He drew her even closer until her rounded softness was molded to his hard length like sweet butter melting and flowing against hot steel. Her senses throbbed dangerously at every point where their bodies touched and moved against one another in the maddeningly slow dance orchestrated by the pressure of his thighs against hers.

Without warning he reached around to encircle her waist completely with his arm, freeing one hand to catch her fingers and slide them up to his neck until they brushed the thick hair curling over the collar of his shirt. Then his hand moved down the length of her curving arm to her side, fingertips brushing each rib beneath her soft sweater before coming to rest high on her hip. Tongues of fire licked at her senses, replacing her tranquility with a swelling bud of desire that she was powerless to quell, even though her rational mind told her that he had intended her to respond in exactly that manner.

The melody ended at last and she drew away from

him, half-reluctantly and half-angrily, hating herself for her weakness almost as much as she hated him for revealing it. She would rob him of his petty triumph if she could. "Is that what you call challenge—demonstrating your manliness on the dance floor?" The words were spoken so softly that they were almost a whisper. "Here in the Arctic we measure a man by his raw nerve behind the control stick of a plane. You haven't shown you're capable of anything, Greenslade, besides slick bravado."

His eyes narrowed. "You'll find out soon enough what I can do, Mickie."

She turned on her heel and strode off the dance floor, returning to the table where a grilled reindeer steak and potato salad had been set down at her place. She ate hungrily, not daring to look up from her plate in case she should meet Matt's eyes.

Mickie stood before the old-fashioned dresser mirror, combing out the coppery tendrils that were still damp from the shower. Staring beyond her upraised arm she caught the high-gloss reflection of two dozen photographs pinned up neatly above the bed. Sally Chandler was evidently an ardent fan of glamorous movie stars.

Mickie's bemused gray eyes focused once more on her own revealing reflection in the glass. Even the borrowed negligee she wore seemed to reflect the girl's starry-eyed fantasy. Mickie had demurred when Lil Chandler had lifted out the frothy peignoir from her daughter's over-flowing closet, but the blonde tavern keeper had insisted with a rueful laugh. "Go on and wear it! I guess working in this town and this old tavern is too drab and unromantic for a young girl. Sally's made another world up here for herself and she has fun with it. You might as well, too. Besides," Lil had added, with a discerning smile, "you look as though you could do with a little pampering."

Swirling the dark green Chinese silk around her and

feeling the delicious swish of it against her skin, Mickie had to admit that it was indeed fun and quite a change from her usual nighttime attire of practical long johns. She came to a stop once more before the long mirror, hands rising to the plunging neckline with its cream-colored inset of lace that was the barest compromise to modesty.

Then she turned away from the mirror and padded barefoot over the carpet to the bed with its coverlet of pink satin. As she pulled back the top sheet Mickie half-expected to find a heart-shaped box of chocolates nestled among the pillows. The luxurious, frilly bedroom was a sharp contrast to the smoke-filled tavern below, where cards were being shuffled and dealt across the scarred tabletops by calloused hands.

Suddenly, unbidden, Matt Greenslade's hawklike profile rose in her mind and Mickie realized that he fit into that rough world downstairs. Despite the good-natured joshing that the other pilots had given him over dinner, Mickie had read the tacit approval of him in their eyes. Perhaps that was what had impelled her to try to make him look like an unwanted outsider. She couldn't bear the thought that he had fit in so easily, nor could she admit to herself that what had motivated her spiteful behavior was a thoroughly childish jealousy.

She tossed the magazine she'd picked up from the nightstand toward the foot of the bed. Her eyes swam with exhaustion after the long day, but she was too keyed up to sleep. Her thoughts kept returning to Matt Greenslade. From the outset she'd known that the man would be a threat to her stubborn independence, but what Mickie hadn't counted on was the subtle but devastating impact of his maleness. She felt as if she were being forced to erect barrier after barrier against his advances. Just how far would he push her? she wondered moodily.

A sharp knock at the door brought her swiftly to her feet and she hurried across the room to answer it. Lil had promised to come upstairs and chat for a while, and Mickie was looking forward to reminiscing.

But her smile fled as she opened the door to find herself standing face to face with Matt Greenslade, his expression glacial and hard.

"What do you want, Greenslade?" she whispered up at him, angry at herself for the tremulous note that had crept into her voice.

She attempted to block his entry with her silk-clad form, but he easily brushed past her into the warm bedroom. Mickie noticed then that he carried a small pitcher and two glasses. "I ran into Lil Chandler at the base of the stairs and I relieved her of these," he began casually. "I explained to her that you and I had some unfinished business to discuss. She understood."

Mickie hadn't moved from the open doorway. "What do you mean?" she demanded angrily, her face red with indignation.

"Close the door, will you? There's a nasty draft coming in," he ordered casually, ignoring her outrage as he glanced around for a place to set the glasses.

"I swear I'll scream if you don't get out immediately."

"Go ahead, Mickie." He turned to regard her and she saw the hard glint of topaz in his eyes. "The guys downstairs'd love it if they thought you were getting the taming you deserve," he remarked almost pleasantly.

She slammed the door, feeling the color in her cheeks deepen to hot carmine.

"That's better." He grinned and held out one of the glasses he'd filled with cider punch. "Now, shall we get down to that unfinished business?"

"You're still talking in riddles," she retorted, moving slowly forward only because there was nowhere she could retreat. Reluctantly she took the glass and waited.

Matt cocked his head down at her and grinned. "You seemed to be enjoying the charade earlier tonight. I came up here now so that we could conclude this little masquerade . . . in private." He held up his own glass and clinked it against hers. "A toast to the consummation of our new partnership."

Mickie was speechless. Her eyes flicked worriedly past his shoulder to the rumpled satin bed. How far did he intend to go with his subtle brand of revenge?

His gaze followed hers and he laughed. "I should drag you over to the bed . . ." He hesitated a long moment before adding, "and turn you over my knee. You've been behaving like an arrogant, spoiled kid all day."

She was mortified at the unexpected drift of the conversation. "How dare you call me spoiled!" Mickie shouted, her long-smoldering temper exploding at last. "I've worked for every last penny I have!"

"That's right," he answered calmly. "But then, when circumstances change and you're forced to adapt to them, instead of giving in graciously you behave like a rebellious little brat."

"You've said quite enough!" she broke in on a rising note of fury.

"No, I haven't." He leaned back against the low dresser, his gaze playing over the auburn tendrils curling around her neck and forehead and the soft curves of her body beneath the rippling green silk. "Since this isn't a marriage I can't demand your loyalty and obedience. But as your boss I think I'm well within my rights to demand a degree of respect."

"Respect has to be earned," she retorted, her eyes like storm-tossed waves in a winter sea. "I can't respect someone I despise." The words were a low, angry hiss.

Greenslade reached out and gripped her wrist so forcefully that the untouched cider in the glass sloshed over the rim. "You speak too quickly in the heat of anger. It makes you say things you don't mean."

"I meant every word I said." Mickie reacted swiftly as his fingers relaxed their grip. She gave a sharp flick to her wrist, the unexpected movement sending the liquid splattering across his features. She watched in fascination as the cider dripped from his black lashes and ran in rivulets down his cheeks.

With slow deliberateness he pulled a handkerchief from his pocket and wiped his face. When he spoke at last his voice was calm, but Mickie's sharp eyes didn't miss the angry tensing of the muscles along his jaw. "I have a theory about you, Mickie. I think you behave like such a brat because no one's ever shown you how to act like a woman." He gripped her elbows and pulled her to him. "You can count this as lesson number one," he murmured as he bent his head and crushed his mouth bruisingly against hers.

He had taken her chin in his rough grasp, so her initial attempts to pull away were as futile as those of a rabbit locked in a hunter's snare. Before the hypnotic onslaught of his kisses she was helpless. Her lips parted and she drank in the tart sweetness of apples, the taste a potent reminder of the anger that had flared briefly, only to be tamed and cast away on a sea of desire.

His mouth plundered hers in a slow ravishment that caused her heart to drum madly. With a sense of shock she felt the uncurling flick of his tongue as it brushed her palate before circling downward to coax her into an intimate duel of give and take. Then shock drowned in the swift, hot surge of feminine instinct and she opened herself to the marauding pressure of his advance. Every sense was heightened, each breath she drew a sweet, soft wind of fire reminding her achingly that she was, before anything else, a woman.

When he sensed her surrender Matt's desire leapt to meet hers. But he'd taken his revenge far enough. The line between victory and surrender was an elusive one. There was too great a chance that he might become the captive. Mickie's womanliness was a potent spur to his male instinct and that was danger. Matt prided himself on his sense of control, on his leaving nothing to chance once a course had been set. Mickie was simply another obstacle he would have to avoid.

Matt reminded himself of that even as the calloused hand that had gripped her relaxed by degrees and began a delicately caressing exploration of her throat, fingers sliding downward over bare skin. His lips reinforced the sensual onslaught, taking a last tiny bite of her lower lip before moving downward in a separate quest of their own. They left their hot, moist brand along the length of her proud jawline to the sensitive hollow behind her ear.

He drank in the warm, gardenia freshness of her skin with a savoring pleasure that wasn't lost on Mickie. Her assaulted senses throbbed and sparkled like the winter aurora.

Their quarrels and her stubborn pride might have been forgotten then, swallowed up in the hungry passion that had begun as a teasing retaliation, but some hard inner core within her resisted. Fluttering her eyes open slowly, she was shocked to see her own reflection in the mirror, bared shoulders half-hidden by the dark profile bent across her breasts. Her lips were red from the melting pressure of his kisses and still parted slightly with the last, lingering traces of desire. She drew a ragged breath and pulled away from his embrace. "I think that's enough," she said breathlessly.

He lifted his head, the hot, golden intensity of his eyes as they held hers sharpening to a hard glint. "Still calling the shots, Mickie? Still wanting to be the one in control?" he taunted her.

She regarded him with anger. "I see. You not only want to own my business, you want to own me as part and parcel of the goods."

"Don't put words in my mouth, Mickie."

She ignored him. "You've had your fun. Now, please get out."

His lips twisted in a mirthless grin. "You know you asked for it, with that clever little toast about Alaskan mountains and Alaskan women. The guys downstairs couldn't resist wagering on how far I'd get with you."

Suddenly it had all become humiliatingly apparent to her. "Of course," she said with a brittle air. "And what will you tell them?"

His eyes filled with subtle mockery. "Good night, Mickie," he bade her softly from the door.

Tears of rage and mortification stung her eyes. "You're a scoundrel, Greenslade!" she cried after him, although she could already hear his muffled footsteps on the stairs.

She picked up the empty cider glass and flung it against the door, where it broke and fell to the floor in a hundred pieces.

3

●●●●●●●●●●●

Mickie rose from the frilly pink satin bed and dressed in the dark, fumbling in her overnight bag for a blouse and sweater to tuck into her jeans. It wasn't until five minutes later, after she'd splashed warm water on her face and was pulling a comb through her hair, that she actually looked at herself in the mirror. Unthinkingly she'd donned a blouse of hunter-green chambray and pulled over it a cream-colored sweater, the combination of colors sharply reminiscent of the lacy peignoir she'd been wearing when Greenslade had barged in the evening before.

Her cheeks flushed at the memory of what had occurred between them and she raised her fingers to her lips, lips that his mouth had explored with such thoroughly wicked mastery. Mickie hated him for what he'd done. Still, she couldn't continue to deny to herself that she'd been aroused by his lips and fingertips against her skin, their effect drugging and as potent as sweet wine.

She shook her head, then frowned at her reflection in the mirror. "Fool!" she whispered to herself. "Don't let him beat you this way." She guessed that, for all his criticism of her as a spoiled and arrogant child, he was just as accustomed to getting his own way. Perhaps she even grudgingly respected him for his strength of will, but that didn't decrease her desire to teach him a lesson or two of her own somehow.

After repacking her overnight bag Mickie made her way down the narrow, dimly lit stairs. In the predawn chill Lil's tavern seemed as gloomily sedate as a funeral parlor. The piano and saxophone were abandoned in the corner, with not even a ghostly echo of the rollicking gaiety that had threatened to lift the roof just a few hours before. She was beginning to wonder if she was the first one up when the strong smell of fresh-perked coffee reached her.

When she poked her head into the kitchen she saw Lil standing before the stove, lowering the gas. "Morning!" Mickie called softly.

The tavern keeper looked up, startled. "Oh! Good morning, Mickie. Did you sleep okay?" she asked a trifle anxiously.

"Yes, fine. It's a very cozy room."

"Good." Lil hesitated. "You didn't mind that Matt brought the cider up to you? He's a pretty forceful man and I wasn't exactly sure of the relationship between you two. . . ." She let the words trail off with an awkward laugh.

Mickie shook her head. "No, of course not. He only stayed a minute," she explained, feeling her cheeks redden.

"Well, good!" Lil replied a trifle too enthusiastically. "Now, why don't you go find yourself a seat in one of the front booths and I'll get breakfast going. Bacon and eggs sound okay?"

"Wonderful," Mickie assented.

She had just pushed away her empty breakfast plate and was finishing her second cup of coffee when she looked up to see Matt Greenslade sliding into the seat opposite her. His boots brushed against hers beneath the table and she drew back as if her feet had touched burning coals. "Won't you join me for breakfast?" she asked sarcastically, turning away from him to stare out the window. Even at eight-thirty in the morning a few stars still winked in the faded charcoal sky.

"I see you're wearing my favorite colors, Mickie," he observed in a teasingly intimate tone. "Although I think I prefer lace to wool."

She glared at him. "Listen to me, Matthew Greenslade, I won't put up—"

Her angry retort was cut off by the complaining creak of the tavern door and a sharp blast of frigid air as the other out-of-town pilots came in, eager for hot coffee and a comfortable booth after having bunked down in the airstrip hangar. Mickie stiffened a little as they entered, dreading their ribald comments on what Matt undoubtedly had told them in colorful detail about their little bedroom encounter. But they had nothing to say beyond a perfunctory "good morning" as they yawned and joked sleepily about the results of the previous night's poker game.

Jake Waller entered the tavern a few minutes later and came over to the table, leaning an arm on the back of the faded maroon booth. "Hi, Mickie. I hear you're flying out this morning. It's a fine dawn, but I've been listening to the weather report on the radio. The storm front's still moving in slowly from the Arctic. Keep an eye on it."

She smiled. "Don't worry, Jake. Caution is my middle name." As she spoke Mickie saw the two men exchange glances. Annoyed, she quickly slid out of the booth. "I'm sure you two have things to talk about, so I'll be on my way. Bye, Jake."

"Remember what I told you," he called after her as she headed toward the kitchen. "Don't work so damned hard."

In the kitchen Mickie bid Lil good-bye, thanking her warmly for the use of the bedroom. She pulled a ten-dollar bill from the pocket of her jeans and held it out to the tavern keeper. "I think this should cover my bill for dinner and breakfast."

Lil raised her hand. "No, no. Put that away. Matt told me he was covering it."

Mickie slipped the bill into the woman's apron pocket and shook her head. "I pay my own way. Bye now, and thanks again."

She heard Lil's voice faintly through the swinging door as she slipped into her parka. "Don't make yourself such a stranger from now on!"

Beyond the flat, gray expanse of Kotzebue Strait the sun rose above the eastern horizon, suffusing the sky with its light. Mickie stood on the wing of the Supercub, dark red curls blowing around her face in the freshening sea wind. She was topping off the wing tanks, methodically filtering the high-octane fuel through a piece of chamois to insure that no water went into her engine. With the approaching storm, temperatures were bound to drop sharply and she didn't want to take the chance of ice crystals forming in the gas line and choking the engine. It was just one of the many precautions that her father had taught her.

Matt arrived as she was finishing up the job and she felt his eyes on her as she worked. Impatiently she brushed the tumbled curls back from her face, but just as swiftly the cold sea wind whipped them forward again. They both looked up toward the concrete airport building as the familiar Jeep came roaring across from the hangar area.

"You two are flying to Russian Harbor, right?" the driver called.

"Eventually," came Matt's easy rejoinder. "What have you got there?"

"They need a few more things and Nome relayed the radio message up here, so we put the stuff together for you to take," the driver explained.

Mickie came forward on the wing as she listened to the man recite the items on the list: evaporated milk, bolts of flannel, flashlights and kerosene. Hearing the list of essential items that they would be delivering to the remote island, Mickie couldn't help but wonder if her new employer might not relent in his decision to cut such flights in the future.

Matt had opened the Cub's cargo space and was loading the supplies inside when the Jeep driver spoke again. "Oh, I almost forgot. They radioed that one of the Eskimos was cut in a hunting accident and they want this delivered." He handed over a hypodermic syringe and a small ampule filled with a clear liquid. "It's antitetanus vaccine from the pharmacy here. There aren't any doctors or nurses out there, so I guess one of you will have to give him the shot."

Mickie paled at the idea; she was barely able to stand getting an injection, let alone having to administer one. To her surprise she heard Matt murmur, "No problem," and she watched as he slipped the small package into the breast pocket of his jacket. Then he turned around to glance up at her. "Ready, Mickie? Let's go."

As the men finished loading the goods Mickie climbed into the cockpit and revved up the engines. She was startled a few minutes later when Matt popped open her door and ordered crisply, "Move over."

"What do you mean?" she asked, wide-eyed.

"I'm flying today."

Her gloved hands gripped the controls stubbornly. "Listen, Greenslade, I know the route better than—"

He bent down to release the catch on her seat belt, then leaned forward over her until his angular, tanned face was just inches from her own. "You're a slow learner, aren't you, Mickie?" he interrupted with deceptive calmness, although his eyes glinted dangerously. "I don't take orders; I give them."

Before she knew what was happening Mickie felt him

lift her easily and set her in the passenger seat. "You rotten bully!" she cried, eyes ablaze. "I think you're despicable."

He ignored her tirade as he climbed in beside her, then adjusted the safety belt. "There's one other thing I want you to know. I own this line now and I pay expenses . . . down to the last broken glass." He reached over, unzipped her parka and deftly slipped her ten-dollar bill into the open throat of her shirt. "You're soft as a kitten to hold, Mickie, but you're more obstinate than any mule I've ever seen."

She pulled out the bill and tossed it to the floor at her feet. Ignoring this display of rage, Matt opened the throttle fully as the Cub glided down the runway.

Their first destination was a nameless promontory that housed a government weather station, several hours north of Point Hope. The weather held windless and clear as Point Hope came into view. If Mickie had been flying alone she would have brought the plane down at the whaling center for a quick visit, but she didn't even bother to suggest that to Matt. She'd already gathered that if the stops weren't profitable and scheduled, he wasn't interested. So they flew over the tiny village, with its sod igloos and air of snowbound desolation, in silence, keeping to their steady northwest course.

By the time they spotted the promontory, with its small, deserted structure, a light turbulence had begun to buffet the plane. Matt brought the Cub lower until it skimmed a hundred feet above the coastal shelf ice. Despite her sulking rage, Mickie couldn't help but notice the tremendous skill with which he flew the plane. He handled it flexibly, ready to swerve gently or dip a wing to survey the undulating terrain below. Unconsciously she held her breath as he brought the craft down until the ground rose to meet their skis and they were neatly traversing the treacherous cracks on the ice. It was a flawless landing.

She said nothing as she reached behind the seat to grab her snowshoes and fasten them to her boots. Matt followed suit and they were soon trekking across the frozen terrain, with Mickie leading the way at a rigorous clomping pace. Within half an hour they'd reached the station, unlocked the metal door and stepped inside. She set to work at once, recording figures from each meter, occasionally flicking a knob or adjusting a dial.

"What's this device?" Matt asked, coming to stand beside her and gesturing toward what looked like two identical thermometers.

"It's a psychrometer, used for measuring air vapor. We usually take that reading in the summer months," she explained tersely.

He seemed genuinely interested in what she was doing. "Where do you send the data once you've collected it?"

"Eventually it all filters in to the National Meteorological Center in Maryland, where most of the weather forecasts for the country originate. This facility is just one of thousands of its substations."

He regarded her inquisitively. "How do you come to know so much about the subject?"

Mickie shrugged. "I studied it for a few years in school."

"Didn't finish?" His eyes weren't taunting, only curious.

"We've all got our priorities, I suppose. After my dad died I decided that mine should be flying. I didn't want to see everything that he'd worked for vanish with his death." Afraid then that she'd revealed rather too much of herself and her dreams to this man, who probably wasn't in the least interested, Mickie terminated the discussion abruptly. "Let's get back to the plane. I'm freezing," she complained.

He grinned. "What did you expect when you took over your father's business—a bed of roses?"

"Not at all, Greenslade." She gave him a look of cool disdain. "I'm a fighter, all the way."

His grin deepened. "Good. I enjoy a good fight. It makes victory all the sweeter."

She glared back at him, annoyed by his cocksure attitude. But the tart riposte on her lips was forgotten as they stepped outside. Looking seaward, Mickie was appalled to see a freezing curtain of sleet moving swiftly toward them.

"Let's go, Mickie!" Matt shouted over the light wind that threatened to grow stronger with each passing minute. "I don't want to be stranded here when that front hits. Maryland might appreciate our firsthand impressions, but I refuse to be a guinea pig, even for your National Weather Service."

Despite his lightly spoken words both he and Mickie were keenly aware of the potential danger they were in. If the violent turbulence engulfed them once they were airborne the fragile Cub could be torn apart. There was nothing more frightening to a pilot then those sheer walls of wind rushing past one another with awesome destructive force.

They were back at the plane within minutes, faces numb from the cold and eyelashes brittle with frost. Matt wasted no time, pushing the throttle fully open so quickly that the Cub shuddered and then rapidly accelerated to lift off the shelf ice in front of the menacing storm front. He banked inland toward the coastal mountains and Mickie knew that he intended to outflank the storm's lower edge before turning seaward again toward Russian Harbor, in the Bering Strait. She would have done exactly the same thing.

The gamble didn't pay off, however, and the plane began to be buffeted by sharp turbulence as the Arctic front edged around them, effectively blocking even an attempt to retrace their flight path to the safe harbor of Kotzebue. He glanced over at Mickie to see how she was weathering the potentially dangerous position. She returned his look steadily, waiting.

"If the visibility gets any worse we're going to have to put her down blindly," he began in a low monotone that was just audible over the laboring throb of the engine in the heavy winds. "But there is another possibility."

Mickie looked up swiftly, but still said nothing.

"The old mine I worked when I first came to Alaska years ago is within an hour of here . . . along the northwestern flank of the mountains. It's a tricky landing site, but I've done it a dozen times." He surprised her by grinning. "Besides, if we make it we can take refuge in the mine itself. It'd be a damn sight better than burrowing down into the snow under the Cub's wings."

She nodded, her eyes weary. "Do we have any other choice?"

Matt directed the Cub's nose eastward and they flew for what seemed an eternity, the rough air nipping threateningly at their tail. "This is it," he said at last, a curious blend of urgency and excitement in his voice.

Mickie sat up stiffly in the passenger seat, staring out through a distorted white world of ice and fog. "You mean where that stand of willows climbs the slope?" she asked, shocked.

"I said it'd be tricky." He grinned again, relishing her disbelief.

Mickie stared over at him incredulously. He actually seemed to be enjoying their harrowing situation. As he brought the Cub down she held her breath, afraid that at any moment the wing tip would catch on the slope and send them cartwheeling across the snowy landscape. At precisely the right instant he tipped up the nose so that the skis touched down at the same angle as the slope and skidded gently upward for a few hundred yards. Then he hauled the throttle back and brought the Cub to a halt just short of a rocky outcropping.

"You certainly seem to have mastered the art of the

Alaskan landing," Mickie commented dryly after a moment, hating for him to see how much she admired his daredevil landing feat. "Have you ever thought of auditioning for an air circus?"

Matt turned to face her, his jaw thrust out aggressively. "Not a bad idea, Mickie. You could come along as my assistant, standing far below in sequined tights."

Her cheeks flushed at his none-too-subtle reminder of her subordinate role.

"I think they'd pay more to see *me* fly and you in the sequined tights," she shot back, eyes flashing with ill-concealed anger at his gibe.

Matt reached out and cupped her chin with his gloved hand. "The circus manager would need a whip and chair, in that case," he said with a grin, "in order to tame your wicked tongue."

Mickie snapped her chin out of his grasp, ready to strike back with another barbed retort of her own. But he had already pushed the door open and the wind eddied about them, its high-pitched roar frustrating any further conversation.

Outside, the plane swayed drunkenly on its landing gear as they worked to secure it with lengths of rope tied to the willows along either side of the makeshift runway. Once the task was done Matt grabbed sleeping bags and a food pack and led the way to the mine opening. He pulled away the frozen boards that partially blocked the entrance and they stumbled inside.

Mickie wrinkled her nose at the musty odor of the cavelike vault which at one time or another must have been a lair for wolverines or wolves seeking shelter during the long Arctic winters. But the mine entrance was dry and provided shelter from the relentless, frigid winds.

After dropping their bags in a corner Matt prowled the perimeters of his old haunt as if he too were a restless tundra wolf. Mickie watched him as he kicked a booted foot aimlessly into a pile of leaves, then wandered over to the edge of the dark tunnel that led down into the bowels of the once-lucrative mine. His restless prowlings proved useful, however, when he came across a stash of kindling and carried it into the midst of the gloomy chamber. "Some Eskimo must have used the mine as a hunting retreat last fall. He left us a little gift."

He mounded the twigs and branches in a neat pyramid, then lit them. The fire created a circle of cozy warmth and Mickie moved toward it eagerly. She turned, startled, as a moment later Matt draped one of the unrolled sleeping bags around her shoulders. Then he leaned down to give her the pack of food and utensils. "Here. Once your hands have thawed you can make a few sandwiches."

She put the things in her lap, then turned to watch as he headed outside. "Where are you going?" she asked, suddenly feeling apprehensive at being left alone in strange surroundings.

Matt spun around. His eyes caught the reflected firelight like molten gold, aglitter with soft mockery. "We should have been stranded together sooner, Mickie. That's the first time you've hinted that you even give a damn whether I live or die."

She turned back to the fire with an angry toss of her head, not deigning to reply as she sliced into the frozen bread with murderous intent.

When he rejoined her a few minutes later the enameled pot in his hand was filled to the brim with snow which he melted over the low fire. After the water had boiled he poured it over the teabags in their waiting tin mugs and handed one across to her. They ate without speaking, the silence broken only by the crackling hiss of the dwindling fire and the low moan of the storm-driven wind beyond the mine entrance.

Mickie glanced over at her companion from time to time, but his features were masked in flickering half-shadows. Once again he seemed to have retreated into the private reaches of his own mind. She couldn't help wondering what his thoughts were telling him.

She leaned forward and drew the sleeping bag more closely around her shoulders. "Greenslade, how did you ever find this mine in the first place?"

He too leaned forward, resting his weight on an elbow as he poked the dying fire. "Do you really want to know, or is this another of the needling exercises that you seem to enjoy so much?"

"I think I have a right to know something about the man who's bought into my business," she retorted, struggling to keep her tone even.

"Fine, but let's make it a bedtime story. Okay?" He got up and strode to the corner, where he'd dropped their gear earlier, and returned with the second down bag. He spread it out near the fire, then came over to Mickie and pulled away the bag she'd been using as a cape.

She watched wide-eyed as he unfastened the zippers and rezipped the two bags . . . together. "What do you think you're doing?" she protested.

"I'm trying to insure our survival through the night," he replied flatly. "It's forty degrees below zero outside. How long do you think it'll take for the temperature to drop inside this mine once the fire's died out?"

"I don't care. I won't share the same bed with you!"

"Fine. Then maybe that flaring Irish temper of yours'll be enough to keep you warm. Good night." He slipped off his boots, slid into the joined bags and folded his jacket beneath his head as a pillow.

For a full five minutes Mickie sat glaring at his long outstretched form and felt the cold inexorably creeping over her. Realizing at last that she had no other choice, she pulled off her boots and reluctantly slid into the sleeping bag beside him.

She lay there quietly, feeling the warmth steal over her where their limbs met. She felt, too, the slow beating of his heart against her back as he turned to draw her more closely toward him. Although she knew that the gesture was a reflex of survival rather than sexual desire Mickie felt her senses quickening at the unwonted physical intimacy. She became intensely aware of his body, its hard yet supple strength molded against her more pliant softness. His breathing ruffled her hair like a gentle spring wind, filling her with a strange, half-languorous excitement. Memories of the way they'd moved together on the dance floor and the hungrily teasing exploration of his mouth against hers flooded her mind. For an instant she forgot that he was nothing more than an arrogant stranger who had intruded into her life. Vital, strong and all male, he'd touched a spark deep in her feminine core. She struggled to quell those treacherous emotions, angry that she should respond so hungrily to his closeness.

"Greenslade?" she said aloud, her voice underlain with annoyance and fear that he might have guessed at her warring feelings.

"What?" he murmured sleepily in reply, the sound muffled against her hair.

"You said you'd tell me something about yourself. I'm still waiting." Her accusing tone successfully masked the inner confusion that she had felt a moment earlier.

"You're a wasp, Mickie, buzzing and stinging without warning."

She felt the low rumble of laughter in his chest and raised her arm, but he had anticipated the movement and swiftly pinned her elbow to her side. He clamped down even more tightly as she attempted to squirm free. "Hold still," he ordered, laughing. "This is a new challenge for me—soothing a thrashing wildcat in a sleeping bag."

She lay still then, almost grateful for her resentful anger which helped to quench the smoldering desire within.

When he began to speak after a moment his voice was low. "I came to Alaska the first time after I'd finished a two-year stint in the Army as a medic. I had all my back pay and wanted to see if I could parlay it into something big. That first winter I worked as an independent contractor, hauling supplies up the Bering coast for the oil exploration companies. I got caught in an avalanche once and had to dig out with my bare hands, and another time I nearly got stranded on an ice flow, when the spring thaw came early and the ice started to break up without warning." He laughed at the remembered brush with danger. "I went home for a while after that to lick my wounds and count my profits."

Mickie envisioned him on the tumbled ice, responding with cool control to the danger and savoring every minute of his adventure. "Where is home?" she asked, suddenly curious to know more.

"San Francisco, I suppose, though I was born and raised in northern Nevada. The Greenslades have had ranch and mining holdings there for three generations. My father and I never quite saw eye to eye. He was—still is—a tough old autocrat, running everything single-handedly. He wanted nothing from his wife and son except for strict obedience. He was furious when I left home and he cut me off without a cent."

Mickie sensed the tautness creeping into his voice as he spoke and she could almost picture the terrible clash of wills between the powerful father and the hardheaded son who refused to yield to him. "Are you still estranged?"

"No. I see the old man about once a year now. We've come to have a grudging respect for one another. He's interested in my business dealings and I think he's even a little proud that I carved out my own niche in frontier mining, although he'll never admit it."

"Surely he treats you as an equal now?" Mickie couldn't resist asking.

His answering laughter was bitter. "He'll never change. If he can't grind his boot one way, then he'll do it another. Last time it was a new tirade: 'Matt, you're thirty-five years old. When the hell are you going to produce some grandsons for me? You're a fool if you can't even do that much.'"

"You've never married, then?" Mickie's voice seemed hushed and small in the mine vault.

He laughed again, the sound this time an explosion of genuine mirth. "What kind of woman would put up with a lonely, hard lifestyle like the one I have up here?"

Nettled, Mickie couldn't keep from replying with defensive spirit, "Plenty of women would!"

"Sure," he assented roughly. "Probably all hellions like you. If I'd wanted a mountain cat I'd have tamed one for a pet."

Mickie twisted around and struggled up in the confining bag, her eyes sparkling down into his with unbridled anger. "Greenslade, you're a contemptible tyrant . . . more of one than your father could ever hope to be!"

He reached up and gripped her elbows, forcing her down onto her back once more. "Don't make me prove it, Mickie," he whispered darkly, his rough-hewn features so close to hers that his breath was like a hot wind fanning her cheeks.

She met his gaze fully, alarm mingling with expectation in the cool, gray depths of her eyes. "You wouldn't dare," she goaded.

"Wouldn't I?"

They stared at one another for a long moment. Her breasts rose and fell against his chest, less from anger than from her heated awareness of their intimate proximity.

"Okay, Greenslade. You've made your point. Physically, you've got me beat. Now, will you get off me?" she demanded through clenched teeth, though there was a breathless catch in her voice.

He grinned. "I don't know if I can trust you, Mickie. A self-centered little hellcat like you might just try to scratch my eyes out as soon as I drifted off to sleep."

"Damn you!" She struggled to free her pinioned arms and attempted to bring one knee up. But Matt had anticipated the move and thrust a hard muscled thigh across her legs. Stubbornly she writhed beneath him, but her struggles only wedged the soft curve of her thighs more intimately into the tight vee of his.

Mickie felt the current of animal heat connecting them, felt the hard, masculine length of him. And the knowledge of his desire whetted her own. There was a savagely sweet sensuality to their contest that rocked them both, causing their eyes to spark off one another in the darkness. Their mingled body heat was a short fuse away from explosion.

Matt's gaze was laughing, hungry. He was used to flirtatious, cheerfully complaisant women, both in business and in bed—not to this hellion fighting him every inch of the way. There was something wild and beautiful to the struggle that added spice to the game and he sensed that Mickie felt it, too.

He lowered his head until his mouth hovered enticingly above hers. "If I took you now, Mickie," he growled softly, hungering for the sweetness of her lips, "you wouldn't fight me."

Aching for the full depth of his kiss, Mickie knew that it was true. "No," she whispered, the circular pout of her lips as they formed the words an unconscious invitation for his questing tongue to invade the softness of her mouth. But she summoned what little will she had left to resist. "No, I wouldn't," she admitted breathlessly. "But I would despise you in the morning."

His answering laughter was low, mocking. "I don't think so, Mickie," he teased, his warm breath feathering her eyelids and cheeks. "I can be a very persuasive man."

"Persuasive?" Her gray eyes darkened in disbelief. "You're a man accustomed to taking, by whatever means he has at his disposal, instead of giving."

"I've lived that way for thirty-five years. Why should I change now?" he needled.

"Because someday someone might just decide to pay you back in your own coin, Greenslade."

Matt grinned at the subtle threat. "Don't play with fire, Mickie," he whispered silkily, "if you're not prepared to accept the consequences." With that his mouth crushed hers with the hard, demanding hunger of a man who knows he's won. But before Mickie could have the satisfaction of twisting her mouth away, he released her. "Now, go to sleep, hellcat," he ordered sharply, his eyes laughing at her.

Long after his breathing had grown deep and even with sleep, Mickie lay there thinking over what he'd told her. His cool strength of will fascinated her. For several years, running her business solo had been the one challenge in Mickie's life. Now she realized that in Matt Greenslade she faced a far more difficult adversary.

4

Mickie awoke almost reluctantly. She had burrowed into her makeshift nest of down, comfortable despite the hard-packed dirt floor beneath her. Gradually she became aware that the space beside her was empty, although still warm from its vanished occupant. Lingering amidst the warmth were traces of Matt's masculine scent which washed over her, a subtle reminder of his physical closeness throughout the long night. The memory evoked a confused stirring of desire and anger.

Fully awake, she turned over restlessly, her eyes catching the tiný patch of blue at the mine entrance. The dimly sunlit chamber was peaceful but for her own thoughts. She couldn't deny that she had wanted him to take her in his arms, to have him crush his mouth against hers in a slow, devouring kiss that banished reason. The spark of physical chemistry between them, ignited by a reckless, two-sided jest, had flared unexpectedly into something more. But rather than softening their stubborn clash of wills, the sexual tension seemed to Mickie to divide even more strongly.

Impatient with her own thoughts, Mickie wriggled out of the down bag and sat up. The frigid morning air was an invigorating tonic that served to clear the remaining cobwebs from her mind. She was lazily brushing out her matted curls when Matt appeared in the mine entrance, stamping snow from his boots.

His eyes roved over her restlessly. "I suppose we can get going now that the bride's awake and the honeymoon is over," he remarked ironically.

Before she had time to compose a suitable retort he had vanished again. Mickie rose swiftly and donned her parka, then unzipped the bags and rolled them into two compact cylinders. Glancing around their bleak haven once more, she saw that Matt had already loaded the rest of their belongings into the Cub and swept away the traces of their visit. Even as she picked up the sleeping bags and hurried outside she heard the Cub's engine revving up. Mickie ran through the soft new powder that had fallen during the night.

Matt was waiting impatiently. He pushed the door open and gave her an arm up into the Cub. "Let's go, Sleeping Beauty. There's an injured man in Russian Harbor who's overdue for a tetanus injection."

She found neither humor nor warmth in his curt tone, nothing but a cold eagerness to get the job done that set her nerves on edge. She glared at him, but was rewarded with nothing more than an impersonal cursory look to make certain that she had buckled in safely before he pulled the throttle back and lifted the Cub from the blinding white snow.

They flew southwest, twice crossing the Noatak River as it wound to the sea. From their height the frozen river was a silvery cord braided with numerous side channels. As they approached the coast the snow gave way to gray-green patches of tundra and muskeg ponds whose surfaces were tinted bronze from algae growth. Mickie found herself enjoying the novelty of being a passenger with nothing more to concentrate on than the patchwork-quilt effect of the starkly beautiful terrain below.

Neither of them spoke until the crumbling, rocky profile of Russian Harbor came into view.

"There's your target, Greenslade, with a couple of inches of water on the landing ice to make it a bit more challenging," Mickie observed dryly.

"No such thing as a routine bush landing, right?" He permitted himself a quick grin. "That's my kind of flying."

He circled the island twice, his practiced eyes taking in the rock-strewn shore below. He flew the Cub seaward and brought it around, dipping low as he skimmed a jagged ice wall. The skis touched down lightly through the shallow meltwater to the shelf ice below. Then he taxied to a stop at the shore's edge.

Mickie felt herself prickling with annoyance at his arrogant self-confidence. "When you're through grinning, maybe we can get on with business," she observed tartly, reaching down to unfasten her safety belt.

He moved swiftly to cover the clasp so that her gloved hand touched his a moment before she withdrew it. He released his own harness, then leaned over toward her. Their gazes bored into one another for several long seconds, hard amber confronting steely flint. "Don't interfere with my small pleasures, Mickie. They're none of your business."

"Small pleasures are for small minds," she shot back childishly. "You're so wrapped up in the cheap thrill of daredevil challenges that you can't think of anything else."

"And what do you think of besides your own little martyrdom at being stuck with me?" His laughter was brief and bitter. "If you don't like it, I'll write out a ten-thousand-dollar check for your share of the company here on the spot. Then you can run back to Nome to lick your wounds and cry foul. Otherwise, you'd better resign yourself to accepting me exactly as I am

. . . small-minded pleasures and all," he concluded sarcastically.

He turned away from her then and Mickie freed the clasp that his hand had guarded with such cool possession. She moved to the rear storage area, releasing her pent-up anger in a burst of energy as she pulled the supply boxes forward. "Take whatever pleasures you like, Greenslade," she retorted, slightly breathless from exertion. "I'll find mine in the faces of the people outside." She tossed her head in the direction of the smiling women and children who had hurried from their homes at the sound of the plane and now waited patiently for their visitors to disembark.

Mickie greeted the beaming Eskimo families on the cold, windy shore and introduced Matt to them. Once the introductions were concluded everyone set to work unloading the Cub and arranging things in the waiting dogsled.

Mickie fell into step beside Nanny Navock, whose husband, Jem, was the headman of the village. The two women walked along in companionable silence at the end of the ragtag procession that wound toward the sod and driftwood bungalows comprising the little town.

"How is everything?" Mickie asked at last, smiling down at the plump, petite woman whose roundness was underscored by the protruding abdomen beneath her parka.

"Oh, just fine." The woman smiled gently in return. "It's always good to see your silver bird flying toward our island." She patted her stomach. "Now that I have another baby on the way it's especially nice to think that Nome isn't so very far from us after all."

They went on to discuss Nanny's pregnancy, with the conversation moving to the other six Navock children, whom Mickie had come to know since she'd begun her regular flights to the island. They paused to wait for Matt to join them outside the Navock home which was tunneled into the sod bank for protection against winter gales.

Once inside they stopped on the storm porch to hang their jackets. The porch, which combined the functions of storage shed and pantry, was the most interesting room in the house to Mickie. She stared at the boots, axes and outboard motors ranged against the walls, along with wooden butter kegs and sacks of apples and potatoes. Underlying the odor of machinery and winter vegetables was the sharper and more pervasive scent of walrus and seal hides. Mickie loved the homely little porch that so neatly illustrated the basis of Eskimo life—resourceful survival in a frozen and sometimes hostile world.

Inside, Nanny led Matt to the seat of honor at the table's head, then excused herself, while Mickie moved automatically toward the warmth of the cast-iron stove in the corner. She wasn't halfway across the room when she felt a pair of small hands grabbing at her legs. She turned around swiftly. "Sarah Jane, hello!" She bent down and lifted the raven-haired toddler in her arms. "You're getting so big, and you look beautiful in those fur leggings."

The two-year-old laughed, suddenly shy. After a moment she looked up again and reached out to touch Mickie's auburn curls which she found fascinating. The gesture served as a reminder to Mickie, who carried the chubby baby to a hide-covered stool beside the stove and sat down. "You know," Mickie smiled. "I told my friend Annie about you and she thought you should have a little red-haired friend of your own to play with all the time." Mickie reached deep into her jeans and retrieved a wrinkled yellow stocking puppet, complete with crimped orange yarn curls, button eyes and movable arms. Then she pulled the doll over her hand and set it to dancing and squeaking in a high voice. Sarah Jane was speechless with amazed delight as the soft yellow arms reached out to hug her neck.

Then Mickie removed the puppet and slipped it over the child's tiny hand. She was thoroughly charmed by the giggly smile that crinkled Sarah's eyes into narrow slits above her fat rosy cheeks. Glancing up, she happened to catch Matt's sardonic eyes on her, and to her chagrin she felt herself blushing beneath his gaze.

In the pleasure of seeing the Navocks again Mickie had almost forgotten him. With perverse illogic she regarded his presence there as a blatant intrusion upon her privacy. She was angered and embarrassed that he had witnessed her playful interchange with Sarah Jane, almost to the same degree that she had been outraged by his intrusion into her bedroom in the Little Arctic Tavern. Both incidents had involved revelations about herself that she had no wish for him to see.

Mickie's attention was caught then by the sound of footsteps. A moment later the Navocks's eldest child, who was sixteen, came shyly into the big central room. Her dark eyes were bright with intelligence.

"Hello, Janet," Mickie greeted the girl cordially, grateful to have her own attention drawn away from the rugged, long-limbed man who sat with booted feet outstretched beside the table. She stood up and set the baby on the floor with her new yarn doll, then reached deep into the back pocket of her jeans. "I have something for you, too." She laughed as she pulled out a long, much-folded envelope. "This is the application you wanted for the nursing program in Anchorage. I asked around town in Nome, as well, and there's a course at the hospital there, if you're interested. It's shorter than the university course and the government would pay most of your tuition, including room and board. I've written the director's name on the front of the envelope."

"Thank you," the girl replied softly.

Nanny returned, carrying a tray laden with fried seal meat and boiled potatoes. "You said the government would help pay?" the woman asked as she set the food on the middle of the table. "If that's so, then he couldn't possibly have any more objections."

"Do you mean Jem?" Mickie asked.

"No, not my husband but his father." Nanny shook her head ruefully. "He doesn't think women should leave the island and their traditional roles."

At those words Mickie pictured Charlie Navock, the oldest man in the village and hence the most respected. He was a feisty codger whose opinions were almost as good as law in the tightly knit Eskimo community. "That's ridiculous," Mickie put in. "I thought the Eskimo woman's responsibility was to do the tasks she knew best. What would be better for Russian Harbor than a nurse?"

"Maybe you should talk to Grandpa Charlie," Janet interposed shyly. "I think he admires you, Mickie."

Matt, who'd been silent throughout the conversation, spoke up suddenly. "That wouldn't surprise me, Janet. Mickie Kilpatrick isn't a woman who's easy to ignore. I wouldn't mind seeing her go a few rounds with your grandfather."

Nanny and her daughter smiled at that. Mickie smiled, too, although her expression was rather less cordial. "I'll bet you're the kind of man who enjoys bearbaiting," she countered with flashing eyes.

Matt bit his lower lip, as if to forestall a smile. "I may have lived in the mountains on and off for several years, but you have to give me credit for being at least a little civilized."

"No chance, Matthew Greenslade," she retorted sharply.

He threw back his head and laughed aloud, but he refused to involve himself in another argument with his hot-tempered associate. When he spoke again it was to address Nanny with a charming smile. "Where are your men anyway, Mrs. Navock? Off chasing walrus?"

She smiled. "Yes. If they shoot another so soon, this hunting season will be a great one."

"Maybe you could take me to the man who was injured in the first hunt?" he asked.

The woman appeared rather abashed at that request. After a moment she explained, "That, too, is my father-in-law Charlie." Nanny sighed. "He cut himself accidentally in the arm with a rusty blade, so we radioed to Nome for the vaccine. Then the second walrus was sighted and he refused to stay behind. He thought it would damage his standing in the community if he waited with the women like a sickly old-timer."

They had just begun to discuss what should be done with the syringe and ampule of vaccine, with Janet hesitantly volunteering to perform the task, when the conversation was interrupted by the arrival of a small boy. Though he chattered in the local dialect Mickie understood enough to pick up that the men had returned from another successful expedition.

The women stood up hurriedly from the table and went to gather their parkas and sharp-bladed knives, for it was their job to skin and butcher the animals that the men had killed.

Mickie stood up, too. "It looks as though you'll get to play medic after all, Greenslade. The hunters have returned."

"I gathered as much."

Nanny came rushing through again, this time with Sarah Jane in her arms. She handed the baby to Mickie. "Would you please watch her for me?"

Mickie smiled. "I'd be delighted to." After the women had hurried away Mickie went out to the storm porch and retrieved her own parka, along with a tiny red one that obviously belonged to Sarah Jane.

As she knelt down to fasten the child's jacket Mickie

glanced up at Matt. "Do you want to come along?" she asked.

He stood up and stretched lazily. "Why not?" he responded. "The past two days have been filled with new experiences for me. Maybe this one will prove to be more to my liking." His eyes mocked her.

Mickie picked up the child and turned on her heel. Before she had walked even two paces beyond the door, however, she felt his hand on her elbow, guiding her down the rough slope. For once she was grateful for his proprietary gesture and did not jerk away in angry rebellion.

The rocky shore was buzzing with activity by the time the two outsiders and their little charge walked up. The crew of Jem Navock's *umiak* had already beached the vessel and were talking animatedly in small groups as the women stripped the rubbery skin from the walrus and set to work butchering the meat. A pair of long tusks were cut free and held out to one of the hunters, who stepped forward with a pleased grin to examine his prize. Because he had fired the first successful shot at the mammoth sea animal the valuable ivory tusks were his to carve.

Moving energetically from group to group, and orchestrating the entire business from butchering the walrus to retelling the details of the kill, was a wiry old man whom Mickie recognized immediately as Charlie Navock. After a while he spotted the three people standing a little off to themselves at the edge of the milling group of villagers and came over. He chucked his granddaughter under the chin, then looked up at Mickie. "It's a fine day. First, me and my son kill a great walrus. Then we come home to the village and see your pretty silver bird on the ice. Did you bring my medicine?" he asked, getting straight to the point.

Mickie gestured with her head over her shoulder. "He has it, Charlie."

The old man turned to stare at Matt, his jaw thrust out aggressively. "You Mickie's new husband?"

Matt grinned, then said, "Sorry to disappoint you, but I'm just the guy who bought into her flying service."

"So she's your new boss!" Charlie cackled at his own joke, his eyes black and hard. "Mickie's tough, like an Eskimo woman."

"You've got it backwards, Navock," Matt retorted with a sardonic grin. "*I* control the Kilpatrick flight service."

Charlie pondered this a moment before thrusting out a gnarled finger and poking Matt's chest. "We'll talk up at the house."

Russian Harbor's festive mood continued unabated in the Navock household. The younger children had been gathered up from the beach and neighbors' homes, while the two eldest boys had returned from the successful hunting expedition with their father and grandfather. The cozy, burrowlike home was throbbing with life.

A natural politician who enjoyed manipulating people and occupying center stage, Charlie insisted that Matt administer the tetanus injection in the main room with everyone present. "Mickie," the old man called over to her imperiously, where she sat at the long plank table with Nanny and her daughters, "come give a hand to your boss."

"I don't like needles, Charlie," she replied. "Besides, you have someone in your own family who's much better suited to the task. Janet even wants to go to the mainland to study nursing. Just think, Charlie, if you had a professional here on the island you wouldn't have to be so dependent on the outside world. She'd have all the basic medicines on hand and could pretty much handle any emergency that came up."

"I can see the women have been talking in your ear," he grumbled, annoyed at not having a comeback for the iron-clad logic of her remarks. After a moment he barked,

"Janet, come over here and help out with this shot business."

After he had held out his arm with exaggerated stoicism and the injection had been administered with swift efficiency before the large, curious audience, Charlie fixed a gimlet eye on his benefactor. "Good. Now that's done we can talk business. Listen, Matthew, you have to fly into Russian Harbor more often. This twice-a-month deal just isn't enough."

Matt leaned forward in his chair, resting his elbows on his knees as he regarded the old man in stony silence. From Mickie's vantage point, the two men with their hard profiles resembled hawks battling one another for mastery of the same terrain. She noticed the subtle muscle-tensing along Matt's jaw and knew immediately that the old man had annoyed him.

When he spoke at last, however, he tried to keep his tone equable. "Why don't you pool your island resources, Charlie? Then you could buy a plane and have one of your village boys trained as a pilot. If you did that you wouldn't have to worry about the erratic schedules of outside bush lines."

The old man jumped up at that, enraged. "You think we're rich like our Eskimo brothers up in Prudhoe Bay with their oil money? Well, we ain't. But no complaints do we have about that. All we need is a more regular connection to the mainland. Mickie's done a good job these past few years, but now that the line's yours we want more regular service. Can you understand?" Charlie punctuated his blunt words by stabbing at the air with a bony index finger.

Matt stood up slowly until he towered over the dictatorial old Eskimo. "I don't tell you how to hunt walrus and I don't tell you how to run your village. You can extend the same courtesy by not telling me how to run my business. Can *you* understand *that?*" His voice was deceptively quiet.

"We want more flights," the old man rejoined stubbornly.

Matt turned away from his inquisitor, his eyes roving to the long table. "Let's go, Mickie," he ordered with curt finality. "I want to get back to Nome tonight to make a few phone calls." Then he strode out of the house without waiting to see if she followed.

Mickie was on the storm porch, hurriedly pulling on her jacket, when Nanny joined her. "Charlie was an old fool to have angered Mr. Greenslade that way," the woman whispered. "When we heard you were in trouble we got worried that your flights would stop. That won't happen, will it?" Her round, black eyes were clouded with concern.

"I don't know." Mickie shrugged helplessly, knowing full well that Matt had planned to cut back on outlying flights even before his confrontation with the despotic old Eskimo.

"But you still have some influence, don't you?" Nanny asked anxiously. "Please try to explain to Mr. Greenslade that we need the service. If you can do this it will be for all our sakes." She ran her hands nervously over her swelling stomach.

Mickie's eyes flashed with new purpose as she turned to face the quietly pleading woman. "I promise you, Nanny, that I'll do my best. Okay?"

Nanny smiled. "Okay. I trust you. Now, go safely," she urged in a soft voice. "He's waiting for you."

Mickie stumbled across the uneven path and ran toward the Cub. Then the stillness of the night was torn by the sputtering roar of the plane's engines and she ran more swiftly.

She barely had time to fasten her seat belt before Matt taxied across the frozen shore, just clearing the jagged ice ridges. Several miles to the west Mickie glimpsed the faint lights of Russia's Siberian islands shining upward through the darkness. Then Matt banked the craft sharply and they were once more bound for their home base on the Alaskan mainland.

Her gaze shifted restlessly from the brilliant panoply of stars overhead to the distant horizon, splashed with the iridescence of the green and white aurora. Despite the beauty of the night Mickie was aware only of the hard profile of the man beside her and of the rash promise she'd made to Nanny Navock.

Within ten minutes the familiar lights of Nome seemed to reach upward to greet them. As the plane touched down lightly on the snowy runway Mickie felt that it had been a lifetime rather than three days since she and Matt had flown out together for the first time.

As the plane slid to a stop beneath the bluish-white runway lights she turned toward her companion. "Greenslade," she began tentatively. She paused for a moment, sighed and began again. "Matt . . . I hope you won't let Charlie Navock's unreasonableness influence you too much. You can't deprive an entire village because of the stubborn foolishness of one old man," she reasoned softly, acutely conscious that for the first time she had called him by his given name.

He stared over at her, the cool amusement in his eyes edged with faint suspicion. "Can't I, Mickie?" he retorted, lips twisted in a bitter grin. "Just watch me. The old guy is a junior tyrant who reminds me very much of another power-wielding old man—my own father. I left Nevada seventeen years ago because I couldn't stand being dictated to. I like it even less now."

"Charlie Navock isn't your father," Mickie argued quietly.

"But he's the same type, Mickie—a manipulator. I refuse to put up with that. End of conversation." With those abrupt words he turned away to flick off the Cub's landing lights.

Mickie's hand reached out to touch his briefly where it rested on the control panel. "Matt, don't you realize you're being as stubborn as he is?"

"You know, this whole Russian Harbor incident has had one definitely positive effect," he said at last, eyes glinting in the darkness.

"What's that?" Mickie asked hopefully.

"It's finally put the two of us on a first-name basis."

Mickie saw his teeth flash against the shadowed planes of his face and she knew he was mocking her. With an effort she suppressed the retort that had risen automatically to her lips. "Good night, Matt," she said pleasantly. "Sweet dreams."

He reached out and cupped her chin in his gloved hand, one long index finger slowly stroking her cheek. "They'll be sweet with the memory of the bed we shared last night," he murmured, the startling intimacy of his words undercut by wry humor. Then his eyes, at once teasing and provocative, sought hers. "You're learning, Mickie," he added softly. "You're learning how to behave more like a woman than a mountain cat, but you've still got a long way to go."

Mickie would have jerked her chin away angrily, but he robbed her of the opportunity by withdrawing his hand first. Before she could think of a suitably cutting retort Matt had pushed the cockpit door open and jumped down to the snowy runway. When she climbed out onto the wing a moment later she saw that he was waiting for her.

Matt's eyes flicked slowly along her jean-clad legs before continuing upward to meet her own stormy gaze. "Need a hand down?" he asked, grinning.

Before she could refuse his offer Mickie felt his large hands encircling her waist as he lifted her down to the ground beside him. "Thanks very much," she told him coolly, "but I don't need your help. I can take care of myself."

"Yes, you've told me that before."

In the instant before he leaned down toward her Mickie caught the teasing glint in his eye. Then his warm lips brushed the corner of her mouth and she felt, with a sense of shock, her own instinctive response. Her full lips parted expectantly as he unhurriedly explored their soft, sensitive contours.

The kiss unleashed a wild tumult of emotion. She remembered the feel of his long muscled limbs sliding against hers on the dance floor, the hot, demanding intimacy of his mouth on her bared shoulders and half-exposed breasts.

Without warning the charged heat of the moment was shattered as Matt drew away from her and whispered laughingly, "Good night, Kilpatrick, and sleep tight." His wry dismissal was accompanied by a friendly, impersonal pat to her bottom.

Aflame with silent rage Mickie hurried across the purple-shadowed snow toward the parking lot. He had toyed with her as callously as a cat teased a mouse before calmly devouring it. And like the mouse she had been helpless in her captor's embrace.

Revving up the engine of her cranky old Jeep, she felt the blaze of anger dissolving again in a flame of desire which rose unbidden from deep within her. She knew instinctively that for all his mockery Matt had been touched by the same charged current of passion.

"Matthew Greenslade," she vowed as she roared along the deserted streets of Nome, "our game of cat-and-mouse has just begun. We'll see who's the prey and who the hunter."

5

Mickie pulled the wicker rocking chair closer to the raised brick hearth, warm from the reflected heat of the coal stove—a relic, like the rest of the house, that had been passed down through two generations.

The entire dining room was veiled in early-morning shadow but for the red-hot glow of the stove. Mickie was in a reflective mood as she rocked slowly and warmed her hands on the cup of hot chocolate that she'd carried from the kitchen. In the stillness of the moment her thoughts moved as hesitantly as the aged wood of the chair, creaking and complaining with each shift.

It was really the first free and unhurried moment she'd had since Matt Greenslade had come into her life. She was forced to admit to herself that he was the most attractive and yet irritating man she had ever met. He was rugged, independent, intelligent and not without a certain charm, Mickie thought as a wry little smile formed on her lips. Perhaps in other circumstances the undeniably potent physical chemistry between them might have led to delightful possibilities.

But her overwhelming need to retain control of her own life and her flying career had been threatened by

Matt Greenslade. Even before she'd met him she had anticipated that threat: It had been evident in his stubborn demand for controlling interest in the bush line. What she had not anticipated, and thus what made the effect all the more devastating, was her traitorous desire to yield physically to him. It was as if her fiercely independent will were being undermined by feminine longing, infinitely more urgent and powerful from having lain dormant for so long.

Mickie's hot temper, never far from erupting, seethed at the practiced way in which he had touched the hidden core of her sensuality. Even though she had been aware on a rational level that he was manipulating her feelings in a coolly calculated way, her body had responded with hungry, primitive need.

Mountain cat, he had called her, because of the way she had fought back, her long-instilled need for self-control and independence battling for supremacy against his subtle yet overwhelming masculine onslaught.

Mickie absentmindedly sipped the warm cocoa, willing her chaotic thoughts into some semblance of order. If she'd had only herself to think of she might have carried on the stubborn, private war indefinitely, taking a childishly perverse delight in her own rebellion. But the Russian Harbor incident and her whispered promise to Nanny had compelled her to reconsider her actions. She needed a new strategy.

Matt's insinuations that her womanly attributes were somehow frozen from disuse had hurt Mickie more than she cared to admit. Angrily she rocked back and forth, though her anger was displaced after a while by anticipation as she put together a tentative plan. She would meet his challenge with a few womanly feints of her own. Perhaps she could gain by subtle persuasion what she had been unable to achieve by willful rebellion. Mickie realized that it would be a dangerous game to play, since her own emotions were so treacherously volatile, yet it was a risk she had to take—both for herself and for her friends in Russian Harbor. Her thoughts were interrupted as she heard her name spoken sharply.

"Mickie! What are you doing sitting here in the dark?" Annie Obluk called from the kitchen doorway. The old Eskimo housekeeper shuffled toward the windows and pulled open the curtains so that the high-ceilinged room was flooded with morning light.

Mickie blinked and turned to regard the woman. "Good morning, Annie. I was just sitting here by the stove thinking things over."

Annie came to stand beside her, patting the girl's shoulder and picking up the empty mug from the hearth. "I didn't see any lights on, so I thought you were still asleep."

Annie lived in the small guest cottage above the garage which she and her husband Tom had shared until his death just six months after Michael Kilpatrick's own passing. The old couple had worked for the Kilpatrick family throughout their half-century of marriage; Annie, now sixty-eight, had helped to raise not only Mickie, but her father as well. Tom had been just as much a part of the family as his wife, even though most of his time had been spent following the reindeer herds over the Seward Peninsula.

The devastating loss of the two men had served to draw Annie and Mickie more closely together. During the four years that followed the old woman had developed an even deeper devotion to her auburn-haired charge. Her love and devotion notwithstanding, however, Annie was always quick to interject her blunt opinions, which were often in opposition to Mickie's own stubborn train of thought. She didn't hesitate to express her feelings as her sharp old gaze took in Mickie's dark-circled eyes. "You should have stayed in bed this morning," Annie admonished. "You look worse than Harold Laws after he's been on a week-long binge."

Mickie laughed at this unflattering comparison to the town's foremost drunk. "Annie, dear, I'd probably have been better off spending the past three days on a Nugget Inn barstool than flying around the Arctic with Matthew Greenslade."

The old woman shook her head in sudden understanding. "So that's it? The new headman is getting to you. Is he as bad as you expected?"

"Much worse," Mickie replied grimly. "He's insufferable and opinionated."

It was Annie's turn to laugh. "Oh! He sounds to me like a man who thinks for himself. You were so used to wrapping Mike and my Tom around your little finger that I bet you can't handle it now when this *cheechako* stands up to you."

"He's not a *cheechako*," Mickie corrected with a sudden flush as she recalled her own incorrect assumption in that regard. "Greenslade has been up here in Alaska for quite a while. In fact, he made his fortune by working a chromite mine in the northern Brooks. God only knows how he found it—the landing strip's like a glacier."

"You were there?" Annie asked, perplexed.

"We were trying to outrun foul weather off Point Hope and had to hole up at the abandoned mine until the storm passed," she explained sheepishly, annoyed at the telltale flush which again suffused her cheeks.

Annie's eyes crinkled with laughter. "I think you're telling me damn little, girl, but never mind! I'm liking the sound of it more and more."

Mickie's brows dipped in annoyance above her clear gray eyes. "Whose side are you on?" she demanded. "I'll tell you one thing that's not going to tickle your fancy. He plans to stop my flights to Russian Harbor."

"Hmmm, that is bad," Annie conceded. "What are you going to do about it?"

"That's what I was mulling over this morning. How could I possibly sleep with that worrying me?"

"Come on, honey," Annie urged more gently. "Let's go into the kitchen and I'll whip you up a Denver omelet just the way you like it. You can't let yourself get run down."

Mickie stood up reluctantly. "I'm not very hungry this morning."

"What!" the old woman almost shouted in disbelief. "Then things have moved even further along than I thought—either you're coming down with something or you're in love."

Mickie walked ahead of Annie into the kitchen. "Don't be ridiculous," she remarked over her shoulder as she opened the refrigerator door. "I'll dice up the ham and green pepper, if you'll start the coffee."

After breakfast Mickie sat alone at the table, sunk in thought. She knew that she hadn't been totally honest with Annie. Her sleeplessness the night before had been only partly a result of her concern about Russian Harbor. Deep down she knew that her fears and uncertainty centered on the changing tenor of her relationship with Matthew Greenslade.

Annie had been right about one thing: Mickie had been thoroughly spoiled by Tom and her father. Whether it was the dime-store candy and toys lavished on her by the devoted old Eskimo herder, or the reluctant acquiescence to her desire for a university education which Michael Kilpatrick had given despite his hope that his daughter would become his flying partner, Mickie had always gotten her way in the long run. But her arguments and stubborn demands had had no effect on Matt Greenslade.

In the cold predawn stillness of the morning Mickie had

decided to take the advice that Matt himself had given her with such disparaging candor. *Try being more of a woman,* he'd advised sardonically. The gauntlet had been flung and Mickie would accept the challenge.

Mickie stared down at the telephone receiver in her hand, then glanced around the neat study that opened off the foyer. She had closed the door firmly behind her before moving toward the phone on the desk, her heart pounding with rather unnecessary force. "This is ridiculous," she whispered fiercely to herself as she dialed the number of the Aurora Hotel. "Why am I so nervous?" A moment later the desk clerk had answered and she asked to be connected with Matt Greenslade's room.

"Hello?" The masculine voice was deep, warm and still husky with sleep.

She took a deep breath before speaking. "Matt? Good morning," she began. "This is Mickie Kilpatrick."

His low, easy laughter sounded clearly over the wire. "I figured that, since all the other women I know would still be in bed at this hour."

What the devil did he mean by that? Mickie wondered angrily, biting her lip in a none-too-subtle reminder to herself that her call was meant as a gesture of goodwill, not an opportunity for more verbal sniping between them. "Listen, Matt," she began softly once again, taking another deep breath before plunging on. "Since we have some free time before flying out again, I thought you might like to . . . to come to my home for dinner this evening. When we first met at the airport you mentioned that you'd admired my father." She paused. "I thought that you might enjoy seeing some of his memorabilia . . . old pictures and whatnot," she concluded rather lamely.

There was the briefest pause at the other end of the wire, then she heard his laughter once again. "Why not?" he replied, voice clear, crisp and obviously wide awake.

"Sounds more appealing than nursing a drink at the hotel bar."

Damn him! she cried to herself. Couldn't he at least pretend to be gracious? Mickie resolutely swallowed her annoyance before speaking again. "Six-thirty, then?"

"Terrific. Shall I bring something?"

"A bottle of white wine would be nice."

His low, expressive voice took on a more intimate quality. "Mmm. The evening sounds promising."

"Maybe you'll like my suggestion less after you've seen the price of wine at the grocery," she retorted, a hint of laughter in her own voice. "Here in Nome we have to pay dearly for small luxuries."

"I can afford it," he said easily. "Maybe I'll bring two bottles."

"No!" Her reply was swift, with an undercurrent of alarm. "That won't be necessary," she added a trifle coldly.

But it was too late. He had detected the subtle note of alarm and could not resist a teasing gibe. "Driven to depths of uncontrollable passion by more than two glasses of wine—is that the weakness I've discovered?" He laughed again and this time the sound had the rough and somewhat reckless quality with which she had become all too familiar in the preceding few days.

"I . . ." she began, intent on informing him with caustic wit that she'd have to fall into much greater senselessness than that created by a little wine if she was to succumb to his charms, but that retort was swallowed as well. "I suppose you'll need my address?" she asked, not waiting for his reply. "The number is one-twelve Front Street. You can't miss the house. It's the crazy Victorian jumble with the Russian cupola and crooked weathervane."

"Sounds intriguing. You must be a real romantic."

"Afraid not." Her reply was brief and acerbic. "It was

my Grandfather Dwight's dream. I'm a realist, like my father."

Matt's reply was brief as well. "A pity. See you tonight, then."

The phone went dead and Mickie replaced her own receiver with a lightly trembling hand. Why had she resorted to such stiffness at the end of their conversation? She adored her home and her grandfather's wild-eyed dream of creating a Nob Hill mansion in miniature on the bleak Arctic permafrost, yet she had been afraid to admit that to Matt. Her defenses were still too strong to let him see beyond her cool, professional façade.

With a sigh she opened her study door and stepped out into the hallway, where Annie stood bent over the entry table, moving a dust cloth energetically over the polished walnut surface. "Annie," she said after a moment, "we're having a guest for dinner."

The old housekeeper straightened up from her task. "I know, girl."

"Were you listening at the door?" Mickie asked accusingly, putting a hand to her hip and cocking her head angrily.

"Of course not," Annie replied with irreproachable dignity, her air of injured pride spoiled somewhat as she added with characteristic honesty, "I didn't need to. I had that figured out before we had our second cups of coffee at breakfast. Now, tell me, do you want to do the shopping or do you want to dust?"

Mickie opened the hall closet and pulled out Annie's colorful parka. Then she took the dust cloth and helped the housekeeper into her jacket. "Why don't you run the errands? I feel like hibernating today."

"Don't want to see your dinner guest before tonight, eh?" Annie asked innocently.

Mickie took the old woman's shoulders and propelled her firmly toward the front door. "Try not to run over too many curbs," Mickie advised. "We just had the wheels aligned."

Annie regarded her with a genuinely injured air. "Listen, my eyes are sharp as ever—better'n a twenty-year-old's. I'm fit as a fiddle."

"Is that so?" Mickie teased. "Why, just this morning when you went off into your weekly lecture about me finding a husband, you told me that you were 'no spring chicken,' and that when you died I'd have no one if I didn't find a man."

Annie turned sharply on the doorstep, ready to take up the old argument with renewed animation. "That's right, my girl. I tell you—"

"Never mind, Annie," Mickie interrupted, laughing in exasperation. "We were talking about your driving anyway."

Annie's black eyes sparkled with youthful indignation against skin that was as brown and wrinkled as a walnut shell. "What's wrong with my driving?"

"Nothing at all, except that you've never quite grasped the difference between a dog team and an automobile. You drive as though you expect the Jeep to remember its own way home."

After Annie had stomped off in indignation Mickie wandered into the living room and attempted to regard it as a stranger might. It was certainly far different than before her father had died. Mickie and Annie had exorcised their sorrow by embarking on a frenzied redecorating scheme that involved plenty of elbow grease and fresh paint.

Mickie's eyes roved affectionately from the Dickensian fireplace, with its black wrought-iron scrollwork and flanking bookshelves, to the walls, adorned with simply framed frontier landscapes.

Through the French doors that connected the living and dining rooms Mickie spied the old white wicker rocking chair, still in front of the corner stove. She hurried over, stopping only long enough to dust the oak sideboard before picking up the rocker and carrying it through the kitchen to the small sun room where both she and Annie indulged their love of plants. Ferns and other tropical plants grew in lush profusion, along with pots of African violets and a pair of delicate orchids that Mickie had coaxed into bloom. The room was an oasis far removed from the bleak, frozen world beyond the cold windowpane, a favorite place for Mickie to sit and dream in the few moments of relaxation she could steal from her exhausting flight schedule.

Deciding finally that she'd dawdled long enough, Mickie embarked on her household chores with energy. Within a few hours every room had been swept, dusted and vacuumed, the plants misted and watered, and split logs carried in from the woodpile. Satisfied at last that the house was as presentable as it would ever be, she went into the kitchen, had some lunch, and began the dinner.

As she worked she recalled her morning conversation with Annie and laughed to herself. "What are you planning for dinner tonight?" she remembered asking casually.

The old woman had shrugged with indifference. "I dunno. A pot of chili, or macaroni and cheese. They're your favorites."

"Yes, they are," Mickie had replied carefully, "but I think I'd like to try something a little different tonight."

Annie had been in a reasonable mood. "Okay. What were you thinking of?"

"Oh, maybe Tunisian lamb, asparagus vinaigrette and chocolate mousse for dessert," Mickie had recited as if she'd been quoting from a gourmet cookbook.

Annie had stared back in speechless amazement. "You're nutty, girl," she observed flatly at last. "What happened to our food budget? What's the matter with

reindeer steaks, or salmon with my home-canned spin-
ach, and blueberries with a little cream for dessert?"

Mickie had finally compromised on the blueberries,
but refused to budge from her main course choices. Even
after Annie had relented with a grumbling, what-new-
kind-of-madness-is-this air, Mickie hadn't been able to
bring herself to confess that she'd planned to invite Matt
Greenslade to dinner, but the wily old housekeeper had
guessed it anyway. "I must have been about as subtle as
an Arctic blizzard," Mickie murmured to herself with a
rueful grin as she covered the sauces, then hurried from
the kitchen to bathe and change for dinner.

As she had done earlier in the living room, Mickie went
through her closet with seemingly new eyes. Even as she
told herself that it didn't really matter what she wore, she
nervously pushed hanger after hanger out of the way,
stopping occasionally to rub the fabric of a certain dress
between her fingers or to reflect on a particular color.

Her closet was jam-packed with lovely garments that
she rarely wore—much to Annie's dismay. The hard-
working old woman pored over fashion magazines the
way Mickie read flying journals and wildlife books, and
she often translated the designs she saw into exquisitely
tailored garments. She sewed for several women in the
community, but was still chagrined that her talents were
wasted on Mickie, who preferred jeans to anything else.

Mickie made her choice at last. She drew out a softly
gathered skirt of white wool with deep side pockets and
paired it with a short, lavender wraparound sweater with
a wide V-neckline that left her graceful throat bare. It had
been made by Annie and, like all Mickie's other sweaters,
it was of *qiviut* which Annie obtained from relatives at
Eelek. Some of her cousins were involved in a government program for scientifically breeding musk-oxen,
once near extinction on the tundra. The animals' under-
wool was softer and finer than the best cashmere.

When Mickie descended the stairs forty-five minutes later she caught a whiff of soy sauce and ginger and knew that Annie had put the lamb on to cook. Mickie walked across the kitchen to the stove and lifted the lid from the bubbling pot, then sniffed appreciatively. "Mmm. This should be quite an interesting dinner."

Annie glanced up at Mickie's approach and for the second time that day was struck dumb with amazement. "Let me look at you, girl," she remarked at last, pulling Mickie into the center of the room to stand in front of the kitchen table. "Pretty as a fashion layout," she breathed, paying Mickie the ultimate compliment. Her black eyes took in everything from the small silver earrings and velvety expanse of throat and bosom to the slender waist.

Mickie glanced down at the simple white pumps she'd put on. "Are my shoes all right, Annie?" she asked. "I haven't worn these since high school graduation, but you said pumps are in fashion again."

"Perfect." The old woman laughed, almost to herself. "Everything is perfect." Annie looked up slyly then, unable to resist adding, "Since you've gone to all the trouble to impress this Matthew Greenslade, why don't you just go the rest of the way and ask him to marry you?"

"Annie," Mickie began, her exasperated tone carrying a hint of warning, "you know very well why I'm putting on this elaborate charade. Matt Greenslade isn't a man who can be told what to do. Maybe he'll respond more favorably to a little . . . friendly persuasion."

Annie's answering laughter was almost a sarcastic cackle. "Honey, you're a smart young thing, or at least you think you are. You know all about planes and the weather and bookkeeping and whatever else you learned at that university. Now, don't misunderstand me. I was glad you went away to Anchorage and I told Michael so, because I knew it would be good for you. But as far as

I'm concerned you left out one of the most important parts of your education."

"If you start harping about men again I'm going to scream," Mickie replied, gray eyes sparkling with the heat of the anticipated battle.

"Men!" Annie rejoined spiritedly. "That's the crux of it, all right. You don't know a thing about them. You can't play them like putty in your hand, working them until they give you what you want. This Greenslade sounds like the kind who'd turn the tables and give you a lot more than you asked for."

"I can handle myself, Annie," Mickie replied frostily.

The old Eskimo woman cackled again. "Sure. Tom and your dad used to call you the Snow Princess, all haughty and cold and upturned nose unless things were going your way. But another woman knows better, Mickie. You just haven't found the right breath of hot wind yet. Then we'll see some melting." Still laughing to herself, Annie left the kitchen.

"Where are you going?" Mickie called after the woman, following her into the hall.

Annie stood at the front door with her parka in hand. "For twenty years I've been playing bingo every Tuesday night and now you ask me where I'm going." She sighed. "You're right about one thing, though, girl. You're going to have one interesting dinner." The feisty old woman stepped out into the darkness, shutting the door firmly behind her.

Mickie's gaze traveled down the long hallway to the dimly lit foyer, her eyes reflecting a strange mixture of panic and relief. However, her panic at the thought of having to face Matt Greenslade alone was supplanted almost immediately by relief that the irrepressible, sharp-tongued housekeeper would not be present to stir the pot . . . in a manner of speaking.

Fifteen minutes later the doorbell rang and Mickie took

her time in answering it, first pausing before the oak-framed mirror to brush back an unruly curl from her forehead. Encircling her throat was a delicate chain from which hung two small concentric circles of silver and mother of pearl. The metal and the opalescent stone seemed to quiver in the light, their iridescence a soft counterpoint to the shadowed cleft between her rounded breasts. She realized with a start that she was trembling from mingled anticipation and fear, and nervously she ran the tip of her tongue over her lips. Berating herself for acting like such a fool, she finally opened the door.

He stood facing her beneath the porch light, his well-muscled form seeming to fill the doorway. Then Mickie noticed the light dusting of snow across his shoulders and black eyelashes, the unmelted flakes catching the light and glinting like diamonds against the curious dark gold of his eyes.

"Matt, come in," she addressed him softly, a tentative smile of welcome not quite lifting the corners of her mouth. "Did you have trouble finding the house?"

He stepped into the foyer, shrugging out of his jacket and laughing down at her. "Nope. There's no way I could've missed it. It's the most interesting bit of architecture on the street. The only thing you didn't prepare me for is that it's so crooked."

She laughed up at him. "Is the house crooked? I guess I don't notice anymore. You know, the permafrost extends several hundred yards below the ground, but the heat from our homes melts the surface layer. It's like living on top of a shifting bed of sand. We're always having to crank up one end of the house or the other. A lot of places are built on rollers now."

"Well, a lot of things are on shaky ground nowadays." His eyes were laughing, and if there was any mockery there it was well hidden.

Mickie hung his jacket in the closet, then turned to

regard her guest. He had set the wine on the table and thrust his hands into the pockets of tight beige cords that seemed to emphasize his tigerish grace. Tucked into the low waistband was a gold cashmere sweater, its V-neck revealing a tangle of black hair that appeared to be still moist from the shower. She tore her eyes from the silky dampness of his chest and looked up into his face. There was no trace of the stubborn, thin-lipped adversary; there was nothing but an easy, almost lighthearted charm that took her aback. Was this the real Matthew Greenslade, or was it but a mask to confuse her and put her off guard?

Rather nonplussed by his manner, she reached over and picked up the wine bottle. Her eyebrows lifted in surprise as she read the label. "Pouilly-Fuissé? I think I've pegged a few of your idiosyncrasies, Matt, but I didn't think extravagance would be one of them."

He reached down and took the chilled bottle, his fingertips negligently brushing hers. "I'm flattered that you were thinking of me at all, Mickie." His voice was husky and low, as it had been that morning on the telephone. "But, actually, I don't consider myself to be extravagant . . . only someone who wants the very best."

"Is that why you bought out the Kilpatrick line, Matt?" she couldn't resist asking.

His eyes roved downward over the soft contours beneath her revealing sweater. "It's not the best," he replied slowly. "But it's getting better."

Mickie's nostrils flared with telltale anger and she longed to slap his face. "Shall we go into the living room?"

With his free hand Matt reached out and caught her wrist loosely, allowing his fingers to move slowly upward until they reached her upper arm. "No. I'll go with you to the kitchen and open this bottle of wine." As he propelled her along the dim hall Mickie was achingly aware of the light pressure of his knuckles against the side of her breast. She beat down the wave of emotion that threatened to play havoc with her carefully laid plans.

Mickie arranged the food on two plates while Matt opened the wine; then they walked back to the living room. "I thought we'd eat here on the low table by the fire," she said over her shoulder.

He eased down gracefully onto one of the pillows scattered before the hearth, then filled two wineglasses and handed one to Mickie. "What shall we drink to?"

"To the successful merger of Kilpatrick and Greenslade," she replied lightly.

His glass clinked gently against hers. "To us."

As they ate the delicious meal his eyes roamed lazily about the room. "I see you're a Charles Russell fan," he observed at last.

Mickie's gaze followed his to the prints on the walls. "Yes. I like the way he painted the American West as something wild and untamed. His prairie scenes remind me a lot of the tundra I grew up with." Turning back to him she caught the coolly measuring look in his eyes as he regarded her.

He reached for the bottle to refill their glasses. When he looked up again his eyes glinted with both amusement and some darker undercurrent. "I can see why you'd like Russell's art. You're a wild thing."

Mickie felt a slow, hot flush spread downward from her cheeks to suffuse the bare expanse of her throat. "Isn't that why you came north, to escape your father's attempts to tame you?"

Matt leaned back against the pillows, propping himself up on one arm while he set his glass on the hearth. "That's one reason," he conceded lazily. "The old man wanted me to become a mining engineer so I could handle the technical end of his empire. I needed action and independence too much to let myself get shoved into the niche he'd carved for me. The adventure and the money inevitably drew me up here, but the more I returned the more I became attracted to it, though someone warned me once that the state is like a fickle woman." He paused and grinned. "She lures you with clear skies and warm breezes; then she goes cold and screams with black, storming fury."

"Yet you came back," she put in, not looking at him.

"I guess you get infected with Alaska's wildness and elemental beauty. After a while it becomes a craving." He grinned in self-deprecation. "It got to the point where I'd walk down the street in San Francisco and begin to feel claustrophobic."

Mickie sensed the tension underlying his quick smile. "So you decided to trade city vistas for raw open spaces?" she probed, suddenly curious to know what motivated him.

"It wasn't as simple as that." Matt reached for his wineglass again, twisting the stem restlessly between his fingers. "I guess I'm one of those men who likes to make quick decisions. I got fed up with company board meetings. And I got tired of having to deal with guys who either didn't know what the hell they wanted or, even worse, the ones who did know what they were after and made a sly game of getting it. I have precious little patience for hypocrites."

He stared moodily into the fire, not noticing the flush that had crept into Mickie's cheeks when he'd said the word hypocrite. He'd told her before that he had no use for game playing; now she feared what his reaction would be if he found out that she was attempting a little retaliatory manipulation of her own.

Matt looked over at her then, the unexpected intensity of his gaze drawing her. He went on, his low voice tense and electric. "Up here there's no pretense . . . nothing but the elements."

"What about people?" she couldn't resist asking.

Matt shrugged impatiently as he raised his glass. "Guess I'm just a loner."

"Just you and the elements," Mickie teased, not quite willing to admit that she felt much the same way about things. She looked into the fire and, after a moment, began to speak. "In a way I think it was that elemental quality of life here that got me interested in studying meteorology. I remember sitting on the porch when I was little and watching the clouds drift in from the sea," she mused, her tongue loosened a little by the wine. "Great rolling stormclouds in summer, or the terrifying winter blizzards sweeping down from the North. Those colliding weather fronts influenced our lives here for weeks at a time. Even as a little kid I was enthralled by it."

"Go back to it, then," Matt put in suddenly. "If I bought out the remainder of your interest in the flight service it'd be more than enough to finance the rest of your training."

Mickie couldn't quite keep the hostility out of her voice when she replied. "You'd love that, wouldn't you, Matt Greenslade? Then you'd have a clear path to do what you damn well please!"

Although Matt still lounged in a half-reclining position, he shifted slightly forward. In that subtle movement Mickie sensed his wary tautness, as if he were a hunter crouched in silence and poised to strike. His eyelids drooped in a curiously self-protective gesture. Though his gaze was half-hidden, the meaning in his tone was sharp and clear. "You seem to forget, Mickie, that no matter what happens, I'll do what I damn well please."

Realizing that her uncontrolled outburst threatened to undermine the whole purpose of the evening, Mickie retreated swiftly. "I'm sorry, Matt," she began, striving to keep her tone light. "My leaving school has been a touchy point between me and Annie, my housekeeper, for a long time," she explained, carefully neglecting to mention that the real crux of the disagreement hinged on

Mickie's not finding a husband while she was there. "Annie thinks I left Anchorage and came home to take on Dad's business out of a sense of guilt."

Matt relaxed once more against the pillow. "Well, did you?" he asked, curious.

"That was part of it, I guess. I'd gone to the university in the first place against his wishes. When he died suddenly, I suppose I felt compelled to take up where he left off."

"Posthumous compliance," Matt observed dryly as he toyed with his wineglass. "That's a hell of a way to get a woman's cooperation. I don't think I'd go so far as to die myself to get it." He shot her a look of dark mischief from beneath his hooded lids.

"I haven't finished making my point," Mickie replied with a brittle air. "I might have returned home initially for all the wrong reasons, but once I got involved in the flight service I came to find that it meant more to me than the theoretical training I was getting in Anchorage. I'm providing a vital service. In a way the Cub is a lifeline to Russian Harbor. If I or someone else didn't fly in they'd eventually be forced to give up their isolated existence. It's happened before. Once the people are relocated to the mainland they have to deal with the gradual breakup of their island culture. Now, after a couple of generations, you find men like Harold Laws."

"Who's he?" Matt asked as he picked up the brass poker and toyed with the burning, half-charred logs in the grate.

Mickie sighed. "He's an extraordinarily talented crafts-man who spends most of his time drunk in local bars. But don't you see my point, Matt?" She leaned forward, resting her hand on the black slate of the hearth, her eyes darkly passionate. "In my own small way I'm fighting to keep that culture alive."

Matt reached out and idly rubbed the soft inner skin of her wrist. "All I see is a very persuasive and attractive advocate," he teased, his fingers performing a delicately sensual figure eight over her sensitive skin.

She pulled her hand away, willing herself to ignore the tingling delight his touch had awakened so easily. "You'll begin to think I've invited you over here on false pretenses," Mickie began, the stiff words imbued with unintended irony. "I promised to show you some of my father's things and all I've done is talk about myself."

"A difficult subject, to be sure," Matt assented with an innocent air.

Mickie stood up, determined to keep her own mettle-some tongue in check. "I'll go get my photo album from the bedroom. If you'd care for an after-dinner brandy there's a bottle in the cupboard above the drawer where you found the corkscrew. I'll be right back."

Mickie entered the large bedroom which always seemed cold no matter how loudly the oil-burning heater off the kitchen clanked and groaned to prove it was functioning. Thinking that it would be nice to dispel some of the chill before she came upstairs again later, she walked over to the corner fireplace and tossed a match into the pile of kindling beneath the log. By the time she had located the photo album the fire had caught fully and was burning with a cheerful radiance.

She turned from the bed, ready to return downstairs with the book, when she looked toward the doorway and gave a startled gasp.

Matt stood lounging against the wooden door frame, the bottle of brandy and two glasses in his hands. "Sorry to startle you. You never gave me a proper tour of your architectural gem, so I thought I'd come up and have a quick look. Do you mind?" he asked casually as his eyes flickered from the high double bed with its old-fashioned coverlet to the crackling fire in the hearth.

"No, of course not," she murmured, struggling to maintain her cool aplomb even as she held the worn leather album to her chest as if it were a shield.

He stepped into the room and set the glasses on a small table adjacent to the fireplace, then poured a tot of brandy into each one. "Who's your friend?" he asked, swirling the potent amber-dark liquid in the bottom of his snifter.

Mickie walked over to join him, perplexed. "What do you mean?" she asked with a polite, uncertain laugh.

He stooped down and scratched the massive shaggy head of her white bearskin rug as if it were still alive. "Him."

She laughed with genuine amusement, kneeling down beside Matt to trace her fingers over the matted, slightly gray fur. "This rug is as old as I am. Annie's husband Tom was out hunting and shot it the day after I was born. It was his present to me." She tapped her fingers reflectively on the black glass eyes. "It's funny, but ever since I can remember I've always felt a little sorry for the bear. I even had a secret name for him—Tajara, after the creek where he was shot." She laughed softly. "He was my protector at night after the lights had been turned off and I concocted all sorts of adventures for us on the frozen winter seas."

"No need to have pitied him," Matt replied, an amused grin lifting the corners of his mouth.

"Why not?" she demanded.

When Matt raised his eyes to hers they were a burnished liquid gold, dark and more potent than the brandy that he touched to his lips. "The polar bear is the slyest and most intelligent animal in the Arctic. You've heard the stories, haven't you, of the Eskimo who was out hunting one only to turn around suddenly and find that the bear was quietly stalking *him?*"

"The man should have been more careful," Mickie observed coolly.

"So should you, Mickie." His reply was rough and quick. "It's time you put away your childhood fantasies and games. You might get into trouble."

"I know what I'm doing." The haughty disdain of her words was undercut by the wild beating of her heart.

"I always play to win, Mickie, no matter what the stakes are." The low, hypnotic timbre of his voice was like soft rain on a shingled roof.

Mickie felt herself drawn to him even as she parried his verbal thrusts with subtly barbed defiance. "I play the same way, Matt. Even if I know you hold the winning hand, I can still bluff like crazy."

His amused grin was a playful taunt. "Maybe it's time we both showed our cards."

He had put down his brandy and his hands were moving up her arms, exploring the softness of her skin through the gossamer wool of her sleeves. His touch was at once caressing and imprisoning, leaving her no option but absolute surrender. She tried to pry his fingers from her arms, but the effort was a futile one. He bent his head toward her, his mouth moving against hers with the insatiable hunger of desire. Then his tongue began a probing exploration of its own. Just as she'd parried his words a moment earlier with bittersweet retorts, the intimate invasion of his tongue was met and challenged by her own.

He pushed her gently until she sat back on the rug, her hands resting slightly behind her on the cold hearthstone. Then he released her arms, one hand loosening the cinched belt at her waist while the other moved with alarming swiftness to push the sweater off her shoulders.

"Matt, please," she begged, her lips like dark, bruised orchids from the crushing onslaught of his kisses, although she herself wasn't certain if she were pleading for him to stop or to move more swiftly to satisfy the growing urgency of her own desires.

His hands pushed down the thin straps of her bra until there was nothing between the naked vulnerability of her shoulders and his inquisitive tongue. His lips moved gently over her breasts until they swelled against their silken bondage. Then his impatient fingers were unfastening the front clasp of the lacy bra.

Thought had fled. Mickie knew nothing but the bright, hot flame of ecstasy his touch ignited. His mouth had found one nipple and brushed its coral tip to aching fullness, and his tongue traced the delicate blue mapping of veins over the soft cream of her skin.

A feline mood crept over her as Matt laid her back against the furred rug and she submitted to his intimate caresses with half-closed eyes. She felt as though she had fallen into a silken net that chafed sensuously against the soft valleys and peaks of her flesh.

"Mickie," he groaned thickly, "you're so soft and pliant. You're not the same woman at all."

Through a haze of passion she heard the husky words and knew that they were true. Never before had she savored the ultimate pleasure of her body as a warm and giving feminine creation. It had been a tool that served her work just as her mind had served her. She had forgotten how to experience pleasure for the simple sake of reveling in it . . . until now.

Beneath Matt's touch her legs became a delicate sculpture of sinew and bone as his fingers molded the curving line of her calf and cupped the roundness of her thighs.

Mickie felt as if she were on the brink of discovery, half-enchanted and half-afraid of these new revelations about herself. In the past her self-image had been tied to a succession of roles—daughter, pilot, student, friend. Now there was nothing but woman and Matt was the catalyst awakening that sensation. As his hands drifted in a maddeningly slow glissando beneath the soft folds of her skirt his mouth recaptured hers in a deep, exploratory kiss.

Had he fallen beneath her spell, or was this a deliberate effort to weaken her defenses, to remind her that her womanliness was a source of weakness rather than strength?

Mickie drew back with slow reluctance from the drugging pressure of his lips and her eyes fluttered open. "Matt, what do you want from me?" she murmured, the words a pensive, half-angry plea. "You've already taken what I valued most—my freedom."

They lay in the flickering light of the fire that cast a rosy glow over her creamy shoulders and breasts and left Matt's features half in shadow. His eyes glinted like amber crystal, their expression unreadable. What *did* he want? Matt asked the question of himself, but it evoked only more questions. If he were to take her now, he didn't know whether it would suffice to quench the raging fire inside him or if it would instead carry him to depths he had never plumbed before.

But Matt was a risk-taker. He always had been. He leaned down to kiss away the uncertainty on her lovely lips, willing to be consumed in the languid fever of their lovemaking. All he knew was that she was the most desirable woman he had ever been with, a woman who touched him so deeply that he had trouble focusing on anything else when she was near.

He slid his hand with slow, caressing pressure along her inner thighs, savoring her skin's tantalizing heat through the silky nylons and feeling his own loins tighten as she moaned against his throat.

The sound of reckless intimacy, fed by the hiss and crackle of the flames and the sweet commingling of their breath, was shattered in an instant by the clamorous ring of the bedside phone. Mickie drew back from him as if she'd been burned.

Still, it took four rings before she was finally able to answer it. Her hand shook as she lifted the receiver, but her voice was collected. "Hello. This is Mickie Kilpatrick."

"You're Mickie?" a languorous, throaty female voice asked in disbelief. "That devil never once told me he was dealing with a woman, but I suppose it figures. How else could he have convinced you to sell your business? That man can have a coaxing way about him, but then I'm sure you've discovered that alreay." The woman's sultry laughter was heavily embroidered with insinuation. "Put him on, will you?"

"Whom are you referring to?" Mickie retorted with icy formality, refusing to acknowledge anything.

"Don't be coy, angel. It's such a bore." The throaty voice was edged with arrogance. "Just put Matt on the phone."

During the brief exchange he had risen from the hearth and come to stand beside Mickie, so she knew even before she handed him the telephone that he had been expecting the call. He sat down on the edge of the bed and lifted the receiver to his ear. "Yeah, Greenslade here."

Mickie went back to stand before the fire, swiftly rearranging the clothing that his practiced hands had loosened with such easy assurance. Over the crackle of the logs she heard his expressive voice, the well-modulated baritone pitched subtly higher in surprise and—Mickie could not be certain—pleasure. "Sondra, hello! I was expecting Jerry to call. . . . Of course I'm delighted. . . . No, not at all. . . ." Matt turned to regard Mickie as she stood alone before the fire. She felt his eyes on her back and she stiffened as his words reached her ears once again. "Yes, she is. . . . Until Thursday, then . . . me too."

He hung up and came to stand beside her. "A pity we were interrupted. Now I'll never know how you intended to play your hand," he whispered, his eyes gleaming like brandy in the firelight.

She turned away from the fire so that her features were half-hidden by shadow. When she looked up again her gaze was cold. "Maybe that's better, after all. We have to leave a few surprises, don't we? Speaking of which," she said, trying to keep her tone light and casual, "what was that phone conversation all about?"

"We fly out to my lodge the day after tomorrow. My manager and a few friends will be there for the opening."

"She's your manager?"

"No, just one of the friends."

"How cozy," Mickie sniped.

Matt grinned. "Are you jealous?"

"Of course not." She shrugged unconcernedly. "It's just that I can't help questioning the wisdom of mixing business with pleasure."

"You hypocrite." His laughter was mocking. "That didn't seem to be bothering you five minutes ago."

"You're awfully sure of yourself, aren't you?" she snapped in return. "What makes you think I felt any pleasure at all?"

"I'd be delighted to prove it to you . . . again." His strong arms reached out to take her, but Mickie stepped back quickly.

"Good night, Matt," she whispered in a coolly dismissing tone.

He came toward her and for one alarming moment she thought he meant to take by force what she now refused to give. But she had underestimated him. He lifted her chin so that she was forced to look directly into his brooding eyes. "I was wrong about you, Mickie. You're very much a woman—passionate and intelligent. I leave it entirely up to you how we work out our relationship. But I warn you: Don't push me too hard or I may turn on you . . . like the polar bear. He gives no quarter to his prey, and neither will I. Good night."

He quickly left the room and Mickie heard the distant slamming of the front door as he let himself out into the frigid darkness. Despite the radiant warmth of the fire before her, she shivered.

6

Mickie left the house even before the sun had risen, intent on avoiding Annie and her sharp-tongued inquiries. The old Jeep sputtered reluctantly in the cold air, but turned over at last.

She drove through the silent, ice-slicked town, heading for the turnoff that led to Basin Creek, fifteen miles away. A thriving mining center during the height of Nome's gold rush days, it had been saved from becoming a ghost town by the tourists who now came every year to pan for nuggets and discover for themselves what gold fever was all about.

As she drove across the barren landscape Mickie thought about Matt's words of the night before, the softly brandished threats that had left her in a cold, unsettled mood. After he'd gone she had climbed into bed, but had been unable to sleep. The whole evening played through her mind again and again. Her openness and candor had been a deliberate effort to disarm Matt, but in doing so she hadn't realized the extent to which she'd risked exposing her vulnerability. Yet he had managed to hold himself aloof from her with teasing words and sensual caresses. She had pleaded her case for Russian Harbor, but in the end his kisses had robbed her words of their meaning. She hoped that she had had some effect on his plans for the bush line, but she was enough of a realist to know that shared intimacies didn't necessarily create shared understandings.

There was still an unbridgeable gulf between them. The life he'd led over the last ten years had made him remote and hard. His stony will would bend for no one.

Although she had been annoyed at the time, Mickie was grateful for the phone call that had jolted her back to sanity. The unknown Sondra had seemed to know Matt intimately, to be all too aware of his penchant for taking everything that a woman was capable of giving and giving precious little in return. She mused on the woman's cynical words while nursing her wounded pride. Did she herself despise Matthew Greenslade because she thought him a scoundrel, or because he was playing the game more cleverly than she was? "Do I even despise him at all?" she asked herself nervously as she clung to the wheel of the Jeep which bounced over the weather-beaten, pockmarked highway.

Mickie hadn't been out to Basin Creek in years, but she had heard that, with the upsurge in gold prices on the world market, some of the dredges were in operation again. She would enjoy visiting Lars Hansen, the man who ran one of the Basin Creek sites. He and Michael Kilpatrick had been good friends, but in recent years Mickie had seen Lars only occasionally, when he came into town for supplies. Besides, she had definitely needed to get away.

It was nearly daylight when she arrived, the sky above the eastern horizon a soft robin's-egg blue. As she climbed down from the Jeep she noticed that the tundra spreading inland from the sea had a few patches of subtle green poking up through the snow. In a few weeks the bleak winter tundra would be a tapestry of colorful wild flowers and lichen. Even though spring was on the verge of blossoming in the Arctic, the morning air was still bitterly cold. Mickie ran toward the small café that had been built at one end of the old mining center. There was no one inside but a drowsy-eyed waitress and a couple of dredge operators nursing a last cup of coffee before heading out.

Mickie was sipping her hot chocolate when the front door opened and she recognized the familiar, snub-nosed profile of Lars Hansen. "Lars! Hello!"

He walked over and shook her hand jovially before slipping into the booth across from her. "How're you doing, Mickie? I saw the Jeep outside, but I didn't know it was yours. What're you doing out here anyway?" he teased.

She crinkled her nose and laughed. "Curiosity, I guess. Still getting a lot of tourists poking around for gold dust?"

"Aw, hell. We're getting more and more all the time—even have them coming in the cold months now. In fact, there's a group coming in today to give it a try before heading on home." The second-generation miner shook his head in mystification. "I still can't get over the fact that people think it's fun."

Mickie smiled. "I think it's the larcenous spirit in us all. I wouldn't mind finding a couple of hefty nuggets so that I could count my money and relax for a while. Maybe I'll find some nuggets today and earn enough to buy back the interest I sold in the bush line," she replied, only half-joking.

Lars's beaming, ruddy face grew sober. "I'd heard the rumors that you had to sell out, Mickie. It's a damn shame. I know that Mike would have hated to see his little Cub in the hands of an outsider. Still, who knows? It just may be the best thing in the long run. I always thought that Mike worked way too hard."

They were still talking a half hour later when an old bus pulled up in front of the café with a dozen men aboard. "Here're my tourists, right on schedule. Would you like to come out to the sluices, Mickie?" Lars asked.

"Yes, sir," she replied snappily. "I'm here for the same reason they are—to have a little fun and take my mind off business."

"Spoken like a true *cheechako*," he joked, holding the door open for her. "Let's get on out there."

Mickie stood at one end of the long trough, dipping her gold pan again and again into the clear, icy water. Lars worked at the far end, washing down the pay dirt with his diesel-powered hydraulic hose and joking with some hunters who'd flown down from Kotzebue. She caught a few flecks of the elusive metal, the gold particles shining brilliantly at the bottom of her pan against the clumped grains of sand. When she had stood there as a nine-year-old she had daydreamed that the nuggets she found would buy a pony for herself and a new plane for her father. Now her musings were more complex and painful. Finally she gave up, her red, chilblained fingers unable to withstand any more exposure to the frigid water.

She retreated to the warmth of the drab café. To her surprise she saw Jake Waller sitting at the counter with a cup of coffee in hand. The grizzled old hunter seemed equally surprised to see her.

"What are you doing here, Jake?" she asked jokingly. "Did you get tired of life inside the Arctic Circle?"

"Hi, kid. Since when have they started a flight service from Nome to Basin Creek?"

Mickie smiled. "You know I didn't fly. I drove here in my Jeep. Where's your plane?"

"In town. I have a small share in a mine hereabouts, so I come down every year to check out my investment. How's that sidekick of yours?"

"I suppose you're referring to Matt Greenslade," she replied stiffly, the smile fading from her lips.

"Is he that bad, kid?" Jake asked, laughing. "He seemed okay to me. He sure took a hell of a ribbing from the rest of us guys."

Mickie ran a finger lightly over the streaked counter top, following the trail with her eyes. "Jake," she began tentatively, "I understand that the group of you at the tavern had a little bet going with Greenslade."

"You aren't peeved about that, are you, kid? You have to admit that all of us, including you, gave him a pretty hard time up there. He deserved a chance to try and even things up a little."

Mickie looked up. "What exactly did he tell you?"

The old hunter scratched his head before replying. "Well, you know, he could have lied and none of us would have been the wiser. But he was honest."

"What did he say?" Mickie asked again, impatience threatening to undermine her studied air of casual indifference.

Jake grinned. "He said you were ornery as a polecat, that you threw a glass of cider in his face and wouldn't let him past the door."

"That's all?" she asked in disbelief.

"Yeah." Suspicion glimmered in his keen blue eyes. "Why? Should he have told us something else?"

"Of course not," Mickie retorted. "Well, it was nice talking to you again, Jake, but I have to get back to Nome."

He tipped his head. "Right, kid. Give my regards to your partner."

Mickie drove back into town slowly, her thoughts a confused muddle. Had Jake lied to her, or had Matt actually said nothing about what had occurred between them in the tavern bedroom? She shook her head, unwilling to believe it of him. Besides, even if he had kept quiet, Mickie decided that he would have done it as a means to his own ends. Matt was far too calculating a man to be trusted, she told herself.

She still had no intention of going home and facing Annie, but one glance at the gas gauge told her that she would have to return to town at least long enough to fill up. Fifteen minutes later she pulled into the station opposite the Aurora Hotel.

She had just inserted the nozzle into the tank when a familiar deep voice rang out behind her. "Why don't you let me do that for you?" As usual, his words were more of a command than a question.

Matt slipped his fingers over hers so that she had no choice but to pull her hand away from the nozzle. She crossed her arms defiantly and stared at the tousled dark hair curling over his jacket collar. "What do you think you're doing?" she demanded.

He glanced over his shoulder at her. "Providing service with a smile, ma'am." He grinned teasingly.

Mickie willed herself to ignore the easy charm which could almost make her forget his arrogance and stubbornness. "I can't escape from your clutches no matter how hard I try," she observed, adding dryly, "Or were you stalking me?"

"I was having a cup of coffee in the hotel restaurant when I saw you pull in." Matt straightened up and returned the hose to the pump. "So I thought I'd come across and say hello."

"Well, hello—and good-bye. If you'll excuse me, I have to pay my bill."

Matt took her arm. "No need to. I already left my credit card with the guy in the office."

"Will you stop paying for things for me!" she railed. "I'm not interested in your largess."

"I thought you might have been out on flight business," he answered easily, releasing his hold on her arm. "At least that's what Annie surmised—that you'd driven to the airstrip."

Mickie forgot her anger momentarily. "Annie? You mean you saw Annie this morning?"

Matt grinned again. "I stopped by your place. She told me that you'd taken off before daylight."

"What else did she tell you?"

"We had a nice long chat over coffee. She has some very definite opinions about things. In fact, she seems almost as stubborn as you are. I don't see how the two of you live under the same roof."

Mickie's eyes flashed. "Well, that's none of your business, is it?"

Matt went on as if she hadn't spoken. "I enjoyed her stories. She also mentioned that she sews most of your clothes. I told her that I admired the soft little wraparound thing you were wearing last night."

Mickie's cheeks flamed. "What else did you—"

She was forced to swallow her outrage as the young gas station attendant ran up with the payment slip. While Matt was busy signing she turned to get into the Jeep, eager to put an end to the conversation.

But by the time she had slid behind the wheel Matt had gone round the vehicle, opened the door on the passenger side, and was leaning across the front seat. "Where are you headed?" he asked pleasantly.

"The old reindeer station at Brevig Mission." She started the engine.

"Mind if I come along?" He slid into the seat without waiting for her reply. "After all, I am a stranger in town and you Alaskans are so hospitable."

Mickie ignored the amused glint in his eyes as she turned to glare at him. "How can you call yourself a stranger?" she asked irritably. "You seem to have found at least one friend in Annie. It sounds as though the two of you got along quite famously this morning. Or you

could start making some of those other female acquaint-
ances in Nome that you told me you hadn't gotten
around to yet."

Matt threw back his head and laughed. "What the hell
would I do with them, Mickie? I can barely handle you."

"You're wrong there, Matt," she retorted swiftly. "You
can't handle me at all." She threw the gearshift into first
and squealed out of the gas station, eyes and cheeks
ablaze with anger.

They drove in silence for more than an hour. Mickie's
anger dissipated gradually as she concentrated on guiding the Jeep along the road that skirted the gently rolling
tundra. The snow-covered dirt trail, for it was little more
than that, began to climb gradually and at the summit
Mickie pulled onto a gravel strip that served as a scenic
viewpoint.

At Basin Creek the morning had dawned with soft
promise. Now that promise was being fulfilled in the
absolute crystalline clarity of early afternoon. Beneath
the cloudless blue sky the snowy tundra stretched away
like a field of diamonds to the banks of the frozen Nome
River.

But Mickie's thoughts were far from the magnificent
scenery below as she turned to regard Matt. "I ran into
Jake Waller this morning up at Basin Creek; he'd come in
with a group of hunters who wanted to try their hand at
gold panning."

"So that's where the rainbow ends." He laughed
softly. "Just north of Nome. Did you find your pot of
gold?"

"No. Those kinds of dreams died a long time ago."
Mickie struggled to keep the sadness out of her voice as
she added crisply, "But I did have an interesting conversation with Jake."

"I'll bet you did." His reply was sharp, but he didn't
look at her. He had leaned forward, his partially hooded
eyes roaming over the vastness beyond the windshield.

"Matt," she began hesitantly, "why didn't you tell Jake and the others what happened between us upstairs in the tavern? It would have been your chance to get royally even with me."

He turned surprised eyes on her. "Are you actually admitting that I had reason to get even with you?"

"I'm not admitting anything!" Mickie almost shouted, pounding her gloved fist in frustration against the steering wheel. "Why do you always have to make things so difficult? I was just asking you a simple question."

His answering laugh was bitter. "How low a scoundrel do you think I am?"

"I don't know," Mickie replied evenly. "I keep waiting for you to show me."

"It's tempting, Mickie. It's damn tempting. I've never known a woman who could so easily bring out the worst in me."

"I can't bring out what isn't there in the first place," Mickie informed him self-righteously.

"Touché, Kilpatrick Junior; touché." His eyes were wide-open and bored into hers with scathing honesty. "But did it ever dawn on you that I've simply been reacting to your hellish temper?"

Mickie surprised them both by her swift and gracious retreat. "Maybe you're right. I'm—I'm sorry. Shall we talk about something other than us for a while? As you so aptly pointed out last night, it can be a rather difficult subject."

He flashed a quick, charming grin at her. "Truce?" he inquired, holding out his hand.

Reluctantly she extended her own until their gloved fingers met. "Okay," she replied, dropping her eyes from his slightly questioning gaze.

The tension was broken completely as they picked up the distant sound of hooves on the tundra below. "Grab the binoculars, will you? They're in the glove compartment." Mickie pushed the door open.

A moment later the two of them were perched side by side on the Jeep's hood, eyes fixed on the scores of reindeer thundering across the frozen river, their herder following close behind in a snowmobile.

Mickie lifted the binoculars to her eyes. "That's Tom's old herd. The man in the snowmobile is his cousin, Jim Obluk." She handed the glasses to Matt.

"God, that's an incredible sight," he said after a while. "This must be a favorite tourist attraction."

Mickie laughed. "It is. I love it, too, even though I've been around it all my life. The reindeer aren't native to Alaska, you know. They were imported from Siberia in the last century."

"They're impressive animals," he replied, turning to follow them with his eyes as they disappeared over a low ridge.

"They are that," Mickie agreed. "But I always cringe when I hear a tourist describing them as cute. They're nothing at all like the ones in the Christmas songs. Reindeer are skittish and ornery. Tom had heard that the Laplanders in Finland were successful in taming them, so he tried for years to tame a few so that they'd draw a sled. He didn't have any luck. Maybe our Alaskan reindeer are an especially stubborn breed."

"That explains your affinity for them, then."

Mickie shot him a look from beneath her coppery lashes. "I thought we had a truce, Matt," she said lightly.

"You're right. Forgive me." After a moment he added, "Are you hungry?"

"It depends on what you've got for us," she said with a laugh.

He reached into the pocket of his suede aviator's jacket and pulled out a chocolate bar which he divided carefully in half.

After she had taken a bite she turned to him. "You know, Matt, this is the second impromptu picnic we've shared."

"When was the first?"

"At your mine." She bit into the chocolate again, still looking at him.

He laughed, the low intimacy of the sound washing over her like a hot breeze. For an instant the surrounding world of rime frost and bone-chilling cold receded and Mickie felt that she could drift forever along the golden shores of his eyes. "How could I have forgotten?" he replied lazily, his gaze moving downward appreciatively over her crossed legs.

He might have reached for her then and she might have gone willingly into his arms, but the stillness was shattered by the distant sound of drumming hooves. Matt glanced up quickly and she followed his gaze. Another herd was approaching across the frozen tundra. Mickie saw at a glance that these weren't reindeer, however, but the larger caribou. The animals appeared to be in headlong flight, but from their vantage point atop the Jeep they couldn't see what the caribou were fleeing from.

Matt raised the binoculars, and after a moment the explanation was on his lips. "Wolves."

She drew in her breath sharply. "Let me see." Mickie took the glasses and focused them on the madly galloping herd. Not far behind came their stalkers, a pack of five lean wolves.

They saw the predators cut out their quarry from the herd—a limping old bull who had lagged behind the rest. She turned her head away swiftly as the wolves brought the injured caribou down.

Matt's eyes, hard and amber-dark with intensity, didn't waver from the scene. "What's the matter, Mickie?" he asked quietly. "Can't you take it? That's the real world down there. The weak don't survive."

She looked over at him sharply. "What's that supposed to mean?" she snapped.

"Nothing at all." His voice was cold and emotionless,

as were his eyes, aeons away from the warm lights that had threatened to engulf her moments earlier. "I was just stating a fact of life."

"You're a hunter, then . . . like the wolf?" she asked, her voice sharp with a breath of fear.

His eyes held hers with the same dark intensity. "In a sense I've been hunting my whole life."

"For what?" Mickie flung back. "Your father's approval?"

"I paid my emotional debt to him a long time ago."

"If you're so damned successful now, then why can't you relax?" Mickie countered softly.

His answering laughter was low and mocking. "Because I found you, lady. You're still trying to get the best of me and I'll be damned if I'm going to let that happen."

Her chin tilted defiantly. "We'll see."

Matt slid down from the hood and lifted her down beside him. "Let's get back to Nome. I wouldn't want to be caught out here after dark." His hard eyes glanced about restlessly. "We'd never survive the night."

She obeyed automatically, her thoughts a confused whirl. Just when it had seemed as if she were drawing closer to him, he had thrown her off balance.

Resolutely she tried again once they'd pulled up into the parking lot of the Aurora Hotel. "Hope you've enjoyed the afternoon, Matt," she said with rather formal politeness, removing her gloves to rub her hands warm.

"Yes, I did." The charming smile was in place again and there were even glints of humor in his eyes.

"You must be looking forward to getting up to your lodge, where you can hunt to your heart's content."

He appeared to relax a little, although his gaze seemed far away. "When I worked the mine, I used to hunt occasionally for food."

"And now?" she asked in a taut, curious voice.

His laughter eased the tension. "I don't have the heart for it—not since I went on a hunting trip to Wyoming a few years back. There was an elk standing motionless on a mountain ridge," he said, vividly recreating the moment for her with his simple words. "I fixed it in my rifle sight and pulled the trigger. When I walked down and saw the elk lying there dead, I didn't feel any pride or excitement . . . just a sense of loss. There's no sport in it for me now."

"Not many men would admit that."

He shrugged. "I don't feel compelled to prove my masculinity with a rifle."

She reached out impulsively and touched the rough, dark planes of his face with her fingertips. "I don't understand you, Matt."

He caught her hand against his cheek and pressed his lips to her inner wrist. "Good," he murmured with a laugh. After a long moment he added, "Will you come in for a drink?"

She pulled her hand away gently. "Thanks for the invitation, but I've got some packing and other chores to take care of, since we're flying out tomorrow." She looked him in the eye. "After leaving the lodge, we *are* flying on to Ugashik, aren't we?"

He opened the door and got out; then, almost as if it were an afterthought, he leaned back inside again. "Let's not plan too far into the future. Okay?"

The door was slammed shut before she had a chance to reply. Perhaps it was better that she had not retorted. Their tentatively made truce was still holding and she vowed to utilize it to full advantage.

7

~~~~~~~~~~~~~~

The icy blizzard that had swept across northwestern Alaska earlier in the week had become nothing more than a memory. For the second morning in a row the sky was a pale wash of blue. It was perfect flying weather: cold, windless and absolutely clear.

Matt was at the controls of the plane, his eyes hidden behind his dark aviator's glasses. Mickie glanced from him to the eastern horizon, where the rising sun caught the white pinnacles of the mountains and softened their jagged outlines with its rosy light. Not far ahead lay Spruce Lodge.

She felt alert and curiously tense, knowing instinctively that the next few days would bring their long-simmering clash of wills to a climax. Would he give in to her softly insistent demands, or would she succumb first, drowning in those amber eyes, that powerful embrace? Even now she felt a treacherous wave of desire wash over her, but she willed it away, recalling again the languorously insinuating voice of the woman on the telephone. Who was she and what did she mean to Matt? Mickie wondered, her curiosity tinged with the faintest wisp of jealousy.

Feeling somewhat uncomfortable with her thoughts,

Mickie shifted in the passenger seat. "Do you think a welcoming committee will rush out to the landing strip to greet us, the way the Eskimos did?" she asked in a teasing voice.

"I doubt it," Matt said with a laugh. "These are sophisticated city dwellers. Somehow I can't see them rushing out into three feet of snow in their expensive après-ski togs just to say hello to me."

Ten minutes later the frozen surface of the lake came into view, while beyond its sloping banks rose the wood and glass structure that Matt had built amidst the encircling forest of spruce. The entire site was bathed in cold shadows because the sun hadn't yet risen above the snowy cliffs that ringed the lake on three sides. Matt brought the plane down smoothly until the skis touched the ice and they taxied to a stop at the shore's edge, fifty yards from the lodge.

Laughing and stumbling, they made their way through the hip-deep snow. Matt pulled open the oak-paneled doors and they went inside, still laughing as they stamped the snow from their boots. Mickie glanced around with interest, her eyes taking in the richly paneled walls and terra-cotta floor tiles. Far above their heads a domed skylight admitted the slowly dawning day.

"Well, what do you think?" Matt asked, a boyish grin transfiguring his hard features for a moment.

Mickie laughed softly as she stepped further into the lodge, craning her neck to take it all in. "What can I say?" she murmured, turning to look at him. "It's stupendous."

Before she could say more there was the sound of eager footsteps in the distance as a tall, dark-haired woman swept around the corner and rushed headlong into Matt's arms. "Matt, darling, you've finally arrived. Alaska is so lonely. I don't know how I stood it until you came!" she cried, twining her arms about his neck.

Then there were more footsteps and the low, laughing banter of men's voices. Even through the amusingly confused babble of introductions Mickie couldn't help noticing as the dark-haired woman pulled Matt's face down to hers and their lips met in a deep, intimate kiss that seemed to block out the laughing, milling people around them. They drew apart at last and Mickie was able to observe the woman a moment longer before they turned to join the group. She wore a bright gypsy outfit, the hem of her swirling skirt just reaching the tops of her pointed, fancywork cowgirl boots. Her black hair fell in a thick cascade down her back, the perfect dramatic foil to her costume.

She turned, as if noticing Mickie's presence for the first time. "And this must be Mickie Kilpatrick," she said at last, her dark gaze skimming dismissingly over Mickie's damp jeans and tousled curls.

"Sondra, right? Matt never did mention your last name . . . or much else about you," Mickie replied, her true meaning like a subtly pointed barb.

Sondra's kohl-rimmed eyes flickered in Matt's direction. "It's Sills, if you must know. But why should Matt have bothered to tell an employee anything at all?"

Their acid interchange was interrupted as Matt turned away from the men and addressed Sondra once again. "Would you mind showing Mickie to her room? She'll probably want to change into some dry clothes after our trudge through the snow."

"Of course, darling," Sondra replied. "We wouldn't want her coming to meals looking like something the cat dragged in."

Mickie's eyes flashed in subtle anger, but she said nothing in reply to Sondra's insulting words, content to bide her time.

Sondra assumed the role of elegant hostess as she led Mickie past the high-ceilinged lounge, with its massive stone fireplace and low windows overlooking lake, trees and icy cliffs. She paused before a long expanse of white wall. "I'm going to have Matt buy a major abstract piece that can make a statement here." She made a sweeping gesture with her arm, the motion causing the heavy gold bracelets on her arm to clank together. "The architecture of this place is superb, of course, but it really does need a designer's touch."

Mickie regarded her curiously. "You're an interior decorator?"

"Designer," Sondra corrected sharply. "Interior designer. Matt doesn't know it yet, but I'm going to put the finishing touches on this lodge—subtle, woman's touches. After all, I am the first woman to have set foot here," she informed Mickie smugly. "I might as well leave my special mark."

"Oh," Mickie interposed with an innocent air. "Didn't Matt mention that I'd been here before?"

"No, he didn't," Sondra replied brittlely, anger and chagrin warring on her heavily made-up features. She stepped aside with an exaggerated air of meek surrender and gestured toward the stairs leading to the guest rooms. "Maybe you should lead the way, then."

Mickie ran up the stairs lightly, a mischievous, unrepentant smile on her lips at the thought of the distorted fact she'd told Sondra. Mickie had no intention of clarifying the matter by explaining that the last time she'd been to Spruce Lake had been years before, when it was nothing but a ramshackle trapper's cabin. She paused at the top of the staircase and waited for Sondra to join her there. "You've known Matt a long time?" Mickie couldn't resist asking as they made their way down the thickly carpeted hall.

"Ages. We've been practically inseparable since I decorated his San Francisco offices two years ago," Sondra replied with a bored, possessive air.

"Yet this is your first visit to Alaska," Mickie observed innocently.

"He may spend months at a time up here in this

godforsaken wilderness, but when he comes home, he comes home to me." Sondra's face had flushed a deep carmine and there was no mistaking the icy challenge in her eyes. They stopped before a door at the end of the hallway. "Well, here's your room. I'll see if there are fresh towels in the linen closet."

When Sondra returned a moment later Mickie was standing before the window, gazing through the trees to the silver Cub. She turned to face the designer. "You know, now that Matt has built this lodge and bought my flight service, he'll be spending more and more time in Alaska."

"Don't bet on it," Sondra retorted. "He's content to let his investments take care of themselves."

"Not in this case, Sondra. He's taken quite a personal interest in the Kilpatrick line and wants to make a lot of changes."

"And I'll bet you can't say no, can you, Mickie?" The woman laughed, a low, sibilant sound that was almost a hiss.

Mickie's temper rose to the surface. "As a matter of fact, Matt and I have had a few disagreements, but I'm quite sure that he'll come round to my way of thinking." It was her turn to speak with a faint air of smugness.

Sondra glanced over at her sharply, as if weighing Mickie's capability for feminine subterfuge. But she seemed to dismiss the thought almost at once, allowing her bored eyes to roam around the room. "I've really got to change these prints," she said, half to herself.

Mickie moved away from the window, noticing for the first time the artwork on the paneled walls. "What's the matter with western landscapes? I love them."

"What sweet, bourgeois taste you have," Sondra replied condescendingly. "That's one thing I have to cure Matt of."

"He chose these prints?" Mickie asked.

"Yes, he and Jerry," she said with a trace of disgust.

"Maybe they reminded him of his boyhood in Nevada," Mickie ventured, secretly amused to find herself defending Matt Greenslade's tastes.

"Listen, angel, I grew up in Nevada, too, and I can tell you that I'd want damn few reminders of it around." Sondra's hard voice was much as it had been on the telephone two nights before. She interrupted her own cynical musings as she watched Mickie unpack her bag. Finally she wandered over, unable to resist touching Mickie's sweaters, which were strewn over the bed. "Cashmere?" she asked casually.

"No, *qiviut*. It's spun from the wool of musk-oxen."

"I'll have to get a few bolts as gifts for my regular clients."

"You can try, but I don't think there's enough spun for export. My Eskimo housekeeper gets the wool from relatives."

Sondra laughed. "It's a pity that such exquisite stuff has to be wasted on frontier women."

"I can't think who deserves it more," Mickie retorted. "We frontier women work hard for everything we have— and we fight to keep it, too."

There was a subtly calculating look in Sondra's eyes as she answered. "I'll remember that, Mickie. Now, if you'll excuse me, I've got to see if the maid has replenished the towel supply in the spa."

Curious as to what the woman meant by "spa," Mickie casually followed her up the stairs.

Sondra paused, her burgundy-stained fingernails curled around the doorknob. "I thought I'd be giving you a tour today, Mickie, but I suppose you and Matt already have taken advantage of this."

When the door swung open it took all of Mickie's acting skill to conceal her surprise as she stared down into the sunken redwood tub. The surrounding glass-domed room, overlooking a primeval world of snow and forest, was warm and humid from the wisps of steam rising from the water surface.

"Matt certainly knows what he wants, doesn't he?" Mickie observed at last.

Sondra's eyes flicked over her disdainfully. "Yes, he does. But sometimes there's no accounting for his tastes."

Tired of exchanging barbed quips with the designer, Mickie turned and fled to the welcome solitude of her own room. After showering she put on her robe and lay down on the bed to think. Though they'd spent less than ten minutes together, Mickie had seen through Sondra right away and found herself despising the woman's artificiality and her dramatically extravagant airs. It was apparent, too, that the designer had set herself the goal of snaring Matt. Remembering their intimate greeting in the hallway, Mickie found herself wondering uneasily whether he would object to being caught. She couldn't admit to herself that her dislike of Sondra might stem from jealousy. She blocked the thought as swiftly as it had arisen, telling herself that she felt nothing more than the competitive urge to rub Sondra's powdered nose in the dirt.

She spent the rest of the morning immersed in a book on wildlife, grateful for anything that would keep her mind from her increasingly entangled relationship with Matt. But over and over again the niggling question rose in the back of her mind: What was Sondra to him?

Restless and driven by her thoughts, Mickie stood up from the bed at last. Though she normally wore little makeup, now she mascaraed her lashes and smudged a bit of shadow onto her lids, the color a subtle echo of the turquoise pullover which she paired with velvety black cords.

Boisterous laughter and shouts echoed along the hall as Mickie made her way toward the main room. As she stood at the threshold of the lounge her eyes were drawn at once to Matt, who stood with one leg propped up on the raised stone hearth as he talked to his friends. His shoulders rippled beneath the soft wool of his Pendleton shirt as he gestured animatedly about something. One of the men said a few words in response, causing Matt to grin and slap his hand against the faded jeans, which were tight across his muscular thighs. Looking at him there before the fire, Mickie saw that he was supremely in his element: a male animal confident in his strength and will, eager to please no one but himself, quick to grin, but equally quick to display anger if wronged. He was, Mickie realized, the most vital and attractive man in the room. Matt saw her then and beckoned her to join him before the fire.

"What were you doing—warming your toes in front of the fireplace in your room?" He grinned down at her as she approached.

"Actually, I didn't need to." Mickie smiled in return. "The whole building is so toasty warm that I don't think I'll be able to stand going back to my drafty old Victorian relic."

"The miracles of solar heating and good insulation. It's even more incredible when you sink down into the redwood tub, feeling hot and wet and thoroughly relaxed, then look up to the glass dome and realize there's less than an inch of glass between you and the sub-zero weather outside," he replied with an easy laugh.

"Matt," she teased in return, "you told me you weren't interested in toys."

"Toys! Mickie, have you ever slipped into a hot tub? One dunk and you'll be convinced it's a necessity." The playful glints in his eyes reflected the laughing exuberance of his voice as he impulsively took her hand. "Come on. I'm going to get you suited up right now and prove it to you."

"Boy, Matt, why don't you spread the wealth around a

little?" The slightly envious voice belonged to Larry Petersen, a chubby-cheeked banker from Los Angeles, with whom Matt had been talking a minute earlier. Petersen's eyes were frankly admiring as they regarded Mickie.

"Keep away from my woman," Matt growled jokingly.

Even though she knew that the words had been spoken in jest Mickie felt her heart beat a little faster with excitement and found herself wishing that she and Matt might have been alone together at the lodge.

Their lively banter was interrupted as Sondra glided up to Matt and slipped her hand into the crook of his arm. Mickie's eyes didn't miss the way she pressed her breast against his bicep while whispering up to him. "Lunch is ready, darling. Shall we all go in?"

The simple meal of crab salad, warm bran muffins and fresh tropical fruits, that must have been airfreighted in, was superb; nevertheless, Mickie found the luncheon a tedious affair. Sondra's hand was evident in the seating arrangement, which placed her rival at the far end of the table. Although Mickie laughed in automatic response to the jokes of Matt's manager Jerry Link, her eyes wandered continuously toward Matt and the woman at his side. At one point Matt caught Mickie's eye and winked at her, but that was the extent of their interchange. Undoubtedly he'd forgotten his teasing invitation to introduce her to the delights of his redwood tub.

There was a brief lull in the conversation as the dishes were cleared from the long teakwood table and hot coffee was poured. Mickie couldn't miss Sondra's coaxing, sultry voice. "Matt, darling, I think it's so thrilling that you have your own bush line now. Won't you take me for a ride in your new plane?"

Mickie glanced sharply from the corner of her eye toward the head of the table, holding her breath as she waited for his response. Then she felt herself prickling with chagrin and annoyance as she observed his shrug and easy grin. "Why not, Sondra? It's a perfect day for sightseeing. Maybe we'll even run up to the old mine that Jerry and I worked."

Sondra's arms went around his neck. "Oh, I'd love it!" She rushed upstairs to change and was back in a few minutes wearing expensive designer jeans beneath her silver fox coat. Playfully she pulled Matt to his feet and a few moments later the massive front doors of the lodge slammed shut.

The lunch party broke up. After politely declining an invitation to play backgammon Mickie poured herself a second cup of coffee and wandered back into the lounge. Less than an hour earlier she'd almost imagined herself to be in love with Matt Greenslade, ready to fall captive to that easy charm. But he had shown himself in his true light once again—arrogant and unmindful of anyone's feelings but his own. He may own the major interest, but the Cub is still part mine! she seethed inwardly, feeling a curious sense of betrayal because he hadn't cleared his flight with her first.

She perched on a leather barstool, only to have her musings interrupted a moment later as Jerry leaned on the bar across from her with a friendly grin. "Hey, Mickie, why so glum?"

Her ears picked up the familiar sounds as the Cub's powerful little engine coughed, sputtered and turned over. Mickie tore her eyes away from the windows and glanced across at Jerry, trying to return his smile. "This is the first time my plane has ever taken off without me," she remarked, careful to keep her tone light.

Jerry laughed. "You don't have to worry about Matt. He's a first-rate pilot. You'll never have to worry about his judgment on anything, either." The admiration and affection in his voice were clearly apparent.

She was curious. "How long have you known Matt?"

"About as long as he's been coming up to Alaska. We first met down in the Aleutians. I'm part Aleut Indian and he's part Paiute, you know, so we had something in common from the start," he explained with a grin.

"No, I didn't know," she murmured. Perhaps that touch of Indian blood explained both his moments of stillness and that hard self-reliance of his which both enraged and intrigued her. She left her own thoughts to pick up the thread of Jerry's conversation.

"As soon as I met the guy I had a feeling he'd be a winner. Matt was just out of the army, with nothing but a couple of thousand bucks in back pay. He was smart and had all that energy—always wanting to do the impossible. At first I thought his schemes were crazy, especially opening up that mine. But he made it all work and made himself a very successful man."

"If he's so rich and successful, why did he bother with my bush line?" Mickie asked irritably.

Jerry laughed. "Because it's more fun for him to build up something old and struggling than to buy a spanking-new Cub from the factory. He loves risk, just the way he loved gambling on chromite. Matt wants to build up the flight service so that the base in Nome is a hub for people flying out to Spruce Lake, whether they're tourists up from Seattle or oil men down from Prudhoe Bay with cash and a little time to spend."

His mention of the chromite mine reminded Mickie that her Cub was headed in that direction at that very minute, with Sondra no doubt sitting as close to Matt as she could, considering that the plane had bucket seats. "How does Sondra fit into Matt's ambitious plans?" Mickie asked with an air of casual indifference.

Jerry squinted thoughtfully, gazing toward the pristine, white landscape beyond the lodge window. "Who knows!" he said, laughing.

"Well, there doesn't seem to be any question in

Sondra's mind," Mickie put in. "She told me that the two of them have been inseparable for the past two years."

"That's not exactly how it's been," Jerry replied ironically. "He spends months at a time away from Frisco."

"How did they meet?" Again Mickie's question was casual.

"Her design services were recommended to Matt through his old man, of all people." He spent a few minutes filling her in on Matt's family and what his childhood had been like. "I think the Sills and Green-slade families had pretty close ties back there in northern Nevada at one time, although I've heard rumors that Sondra's father was the black sheep of the family. In fact, Matt and Sondra knew each other as kids. When they met again a couple of years ago old Greenslade started pushing for a wedding right away." Jerry paused and reached behind him to pick up the glass coffeepot from the hot plate. He refilled Mickie's cup and poured one for himself.

She watched the cream swirl in the black liquid as she slowly stirred it. Looking up at last she asked softly, "What happened?"

Jerry scratched his head with a perplexed air. "I could never figure out if he cooled the affair because of his old man's interference or what. He and Sondra are good friends, though she still has plans for more than that. Her family was real poor and she's had nothing but ambitions to be rich ever since."

"Doesn't Matt see through her?"

"Don't kid yourself. Matt's a sharp guy. The friendship's convenient for them both."

"Friendship," Mickie scoffed with a surprisingly bitter little laugh. "I'd hardly call their hello kiss this morning 'friendly.'"

He grinned. "Sondra's a good-looking woman and Matt craves affection. You know, that's what confuses me." Jerry became serious again. "Beneath it all, I think he wants and needs a woman."

"And Sondra is working hard to provide him with all that he needs," Mickie observed tartly.

Jerry shrugged. "She's trying to, anyway."

The two lapsed into a reflective silence which was broken after a while by a distant howling that slid up the scale in a gathering crescendo. Mickie recognized the peculiar sound at once. "Sled dogs!" she cried eagerly. "Are they based here at the lodge? Matt never mentioned them."

Jerry smiled proudly. "Yeah, that's our own team you hear. Old Bob Kehoe must be heading down to feed them, so they're greeting him. The dogs and the sled are another one of Matt's plans to make this lodge of his something special. Visitors'll be able to get a real authentic feel for what Alaskan life was like before the twentieth century sneaked up with its planes, snowmobiles and oil-drilling equipment. There's a small Eskimo village called Lalak about forty miles from here. People will be able to run out there with a guide, traveling all the way by dogsled."

"Jerry, do you think I could go down to see the dogs? My dad and I used to race a team for fun in Nome." Mickie's eyes were eager and shining with excitement.

Five minutes after Jerry had given her directions on how to find her way down to the dog pen Mickie had slipped into her parka and was standing outside in the clear, frigid air. She easily found the narrow path that Bob Kehoe had shoveled through the massing snowdrifts and followed it to the back of the lodge. As she rounded the corner of the new glass and wood structure Mickie was astonished to find that Harry LaCrosse's quaint one-room shack had been moved back from the lake site and preserved as a kind of whimsical window into the past—the white man's past in Alaska.

Tears started to cloud her eyes as she recalled the last

time she had been to Spruce Lake. She had stopped at the gruff old trapper's cabin for a brief respite from the grueling cross-country dogsled trek and been treated to a cup of his thick, bitter coffee. She pushed through the snow that had drifted against the cabin walls and peered through the window, her nostalgic tears dissolving in silent laughter as she looked at the familiar, battered, enamel coffeepot, still in place atop the rickety iron stove. "Old Harry's spirit'll never die," she murmured aloud, laughing as she moved back along the path that led to a lean-to enclosed with chicken wire. Its sloping roof was piled high with snow.

The dogs leaped against the wire at her approach, howling and crying with delight at this new distraction following so quickly after their midday meal. "Mr. Kehoe!" she called into the dim enclosure.

The wiry old Eskimo straightened up from his task of chopping the ice out of their drinking tub. "Good afternoon, Miss," he replied cordially. "Come in."

Mickie pushed open the enclosure gate and went inside. The dogs crowded up against her, tails wagging as they sniffed at her curiously. She stared down into the alert, friendly blue gazes of the Siberian huskies and the brown eyes of the larger malamutes. "Mr. Kehoe, your dogs are so good-tempered." Mickie laughed as she ran her gloved hands over the thick, soft fur of the animals surrounding her. "They aren't mean and snappy, like a lot I've seen."

He nodded sagely. "They get that way out of boredom, from being tied up for weeks at a time. Every day or so me and my wife Sarah run these fellas up to Lalak or up to a hunting lodge about twenty-five miles from here that Mr. Greenslade bought last year."

"That's terrific," Mickie replied enthusiastically. "They're still work dogs, then. I used to mush when I was in high school in Nome."

Kehoe's seamed, brown face split in a smile of delight

at having found someone to share his interest in the dogs. "You want to go out for a run now?"

Several minutes later the excited animals had been hitched up and Kehoe and Mickie stood behind the sled. The old man graciously handed her the whip which she cracked lightly over the dogs' rumps. Then they were off, with the fierce, cold wind whipping against their cheeks. Kehoe pointed out the path that led to his village before setting the dogs on a course that followed the perimeter of the cliffs behind the lake. The dogs moved into a swift trot that caused the sled to bounce dizzyingly over the packed snow.

Beyond the straining shoulder muscles and alert ears of the dogs Mickie saw Matt's lodge, like an exquisite piece of sculpture rising upward from the snowy lake-shore. The brilliant spring sun caught the black solar panels and clear domes of the skylights until the whole building seemed to shimmer with the intensity of the reflection.

Then the lodge disappeared from view once more as the dogs changed course and Mickie saw and felt nothing but the exhilarating joy of the run. The mood wasn't broken even when her ears picked up the distant drone of the returning Cub. She and Kehoe laughed like mischievous children as the dogs careened madly over the blindingly white snow. Inevitably, however, their play had to end. The old man drew his animals back to a sedate walk and led them panting into their dry enclosure. He hurried back up to the lodge to do his other chores, but Mickie lingered a while longer.

She was standing outside the dogs' enclosure when she heard the loud drone of the Cub circling overhead. A moment later it had touched down on the icy lake surface with a light bump. Mickie was debating whether to greet the returning couple when she heard a noise behind her and glanced up. Two seconds later she drew in a freezing gasp of snow as a great white mass of powder, loosened from its mooring on the sloping shed roof, slid forward and drenched her in an icy bath. Shocked and gasping, Mickie shook herself free and made her way up the slippery back path to the lodge as quickly as her heavy clothing would permit.

She had just rounded the corner and was hurrying toward the front door when Matt and Sondra appeared. Mickie would have turned and retreated until they had gone safely into the lodge, but it was too late. They had seen her. She had no choice but to continue on with as much dignity as she could muster.

They stopped and waited for her on the wide flagstone steps. As she approached Mickie was all too aware of the ridiculous picture she must be presenting: a bedraggled snow-woman with wet, stringy hair and lips blue from the cold.

"What the devil happened to you, Mickie?" Matt asked finally, his eyes expressing a curious mixture of amusement and concern.

"Oh," she replied with an unsuccessful attempt at airiness as she lifted the sodden arm of her parka, "I thought I'd try that old Finnish custom of rolling in the snow. They say it does wonders for the complexion." Her cheeks were numb and her teeth chattered uncontrollably.

Matt took her arm and pulled her into the skylit warmth of the lodge entry. "The Finns usually take their roll in the snow naked, after they've been baking in a sauna," he said dryly, reaching out to unzip her parka and strip it from her shoulders.

She submitted unprotestingly to his assistance.

"So much for the wonder woman of the North," Sondra teased, giggling nastily as she followed them inside. "She looks more like the abominable snowman."

Mickie flashed her an angry look, noticing resentfully that not a strand of her coiled black hair was out of place and that her expensive tooled-leather boots were barely moist after her trek up from the lakeshore.

"What really happened to you?" Matt asked, catching the corner of his lip with his teeth to keep from grinning.

"Bob Kehoe and I went out for a dogsled run. Afterward I was standing in front of the lean-to when the snow on the roof loosened and cascaded over my head," she explained, grateful that the bright rosiness of her cheeks would be taken as a sign of chill rather than acute embarrassment.

Sondra put her hand on Matt's sleeve. "Come on, darling, let's have a glass of sherry before the fire. I'm sure it'll be a while before Mickie can make herself presentable." She cast a final, disdainful glance in Mickie's direction before moving down the hallway, her high boot heels clicking sharply on the tiles.

"Would you like me to see you up to your room?" Matt asked, his eyes warm and teasing as they flickered down her figure. "A rubdown can do wonders for cold muscles."

"Is that part of the Spruce Lodge package you offer all your guests?" she flung back, still annoyed that he'd taken Sondra up in the Cub.

His gaze flickered over the rise of her breasts as she reached up to unwind her muffler. "I'm not interested in package deals, Mickie. The bargain is illusory and you always wind up paying far more than they're worth." There was a cutting edge to his voice that caused Mickie's head to snap up.

"If you're not satisfied with the deal, then maybe you should reconsider your offer," she replied coolly, knowing full well that his gibe had been directed at their fledgling partnership in the bush line.

His answering grin was quick and mischievous. "Not until I've weighed all the intangible benefits."

Mickie went pink at that. "I doubt if you know the

meaning of intangibles," she accused to hide her confusion. "All you're really interested in are the cold facts of cash flow and profit margin."

"Business is business where I'm concerned, is that it, Mickie?" he needled. "Is that all you see in me?"

"That's all you've shown me."

"Liar," he riposted softly, the look of wicked, knowing amusement in his eyes sending an unexpected flood of sensual awareness along her limbs.

Without replying she turned on her heel and climbed the stairs, burningly aware of his gaze on the feminine twitch of her hips with each step she took.

An hour later, after a long hot soak in the tub, Mickie stood drying off before the warmth of the blaze in her bedroom grate. She looked up, startled, when someone knocked on the door.

"Who is it?" she demanded as she flung aside the towel and slipped hurriedly into her thin white robe.

"Matt."

The low, familiar voice sent a tremor through her and Mickie reached up with nervous fingers to smooth out the wet tumble of curls on her head.

She opened the door slowly, eyeing him from beneath her lashes with a rueful, not quite trusting expression. "What is it now, Greenslade?" A faint, wry smile turned up the corners of her lips.

He held up the thermos and two mugs he was carrying. "Just thought you could use some hot coffee."

She stepped back and Matt took it as an invitation. Mickie followed his gaze as it touched the damp towel on the hearth and the twist of pale lace panties against the dark armchair where she'd casually flung them. Then his eyes roved to the fragrant mist spilling out from the bathroom before turning back to her.

"Guess I'm too late to scrub your back," he observed with teasing disappointment.

The beguiling intimacy of their situation, with her

clothing flung about the room and Matt casually pouring coffee at the fireplace mantel, touched Mickie. For one foolish moment she wished it could always be that way. But, seductive as the notion was, they could never be lovers or even friends, not as long as he was a threat to the distant villagers whose lives depended on her flight service. They were adversaries, reluctant partners in a shaky business proposition.

Afraid that he might have sensed her fleeting vulnerability, Mickie set her lips in a cool, disciplined line as she went to join him. "Why did you come up here, Matt? Have you already gotten bored with Sondra?"

He cocked his head interestedly. "Jealous, Mickie?" he teased.

"Hardly." Without looking at him she took the mug he held out and went to curl up on the deep windowsill. "As a matter of fact, I think she's just your type," she couldn't resist sniping.

From beneath her lashes she watched him pick up the little triangle of lace and toss it onto the bed before settling down in the armchair, with his long legs stretched out in front of the fire. "Sondra and I do have one thing in common," Matt agreed lazily. "A healthy self-interest."

"Don't we all?" Mickie murmured half to herself, gazing out over the frozen landscape and thinking of the brave promise she had made to Nanny Navock. Her concern for the villagers' future hadn't been her sole motivation. She had also needed to assuage her bruised pride, to prove to the world that she still had some shred of control. And she was using Matt to prove it, to exact her revenge.

He regarded her inquisitively while the thoughts were rushing pell-mell through her head. His eyes took in the brush of wet curls, dark as mahogany against her pale cheeks, and the stubborn, faintly pouting lips that gave her a look of tough innocence. Even as his gaze swept down appreciatively over the sweet curve of her breasts beneath the thin wool, the thought struck him that she was a woman he could trust. He'd said that about very few people in his life, but some gut-level instinct told him that Mickie Kilpatrick was different . . . special.

He broke into his own bemused thoughts by asking aloud, "What are you thinking, Mickie?"

She glanced around in surprise, warmed by the husky baritone that seemed to reach across to her. Gone was the strident arrogance that had grated on her pride and she wasn't quite certain how to reply. "I . . ." she began uncertainly, breaking off to stare outside again with a little frown of perplexity.

"Are you regretting that the Cub's not yours anymore?" he asked curiously.

Mickie sighed. "You can't turn the clock back."

"Are you wishing I hadn't barged into your life?" he persisted.

She turned slowly to regard him again, her gray eyes faintly troubled and brooding. "I don't know the answer to that, either, Matt." Their eyes met and held for a fragile instant. Then she took refuge in the steaming coffee that she raised to her lips. "By the way, thanks for this," she said finally. "It's really warmed my insides. I felt like ice before."

Matt stood up and with a wry smile sauntered over toward her. "Ice Princess," he teased softly. "I hear that was your nickname."

She tried to ignore the flutter of excitement that wafted through her at his closeness. He had leaned one shoulder against the wall and was laughing down at her.

She tossed her head back with a mock indifferent shrug that fooled neither of them. "What else did Annie tell you?"

"That it would take one hell of a man to tame you." His eyes caressed her mouth with a look more headily potent than any kiss.

Mickie drew in a trembling breath. "She's got her nerve," she bridled softly.

Reluctantly he lifted his eyes from the seductive pout of her lips to pin her with an amused stare. "It isn't true, then?"

She laughed in the same soft voice, a low, resonant exhalation that echoed between them. "It's true."

"You shouldn't have admitted that, Mickie," he whispered. "You should know by now that I'm the kind of man who can't ignore a challenge like that." His eyes traveled down the curves of her body as if they possessed the power to brush aside the cloth and touch the silken dampness of her naked skin.

His words and the visual caress washed over in a hot wave that threatened to swallow her, but she fought the devastating impact of his maleness. "Aren't you afraid of losing sometime?" she asked in a deceptively cool voice.

He cocked his head at a lazy, arrogant tilt. "Aren't you?"

She looked out the window again, afraid that he would sense the silent battle raging within her. Gratefully she focused on the figure of Sarah Kehoe, wrapped in a bulky anorak. The Eskimo woman trudged through the snow to the lake's edge, a short-handled ax resting on one shoulder.

Matt followed her gaze. "They're tough people," he remarked at last.

A faint smile curved Mickie's lips as she looked up at him. "They're just as vulnerable as the rest of us—as you and I."

He shook his head. "You're wrong about me, Mickie."

"Am I?" She laughed softly, aware that the subtle movement of her body had caused the hem of her gown to slide away from the shadowed curve of her legs.

Her heart pounded in reckless rhythm as she heard his sharp intake of breath and felt the hungry sweep of his eyes along her bared limbs. In a rush of joy she closed her eyes, savoring the gentle pressure of his fingertips against her throat as he leaned down to brush her lips with his own. The teasingly feathered kiss breathed a promise of passion, but no more than that. Almost as soon as it had begun, it was over. He straightened up and stared down at her with a look of amused regret. "Glad to see my coffee warmed you up," he teased in a husky whisper. "But, unfortunately, I can't stick around to enjoy the aftereffects. I've got a business to run and obligations downstairs. See you at dinner."

He was gone before she could say anything, leaving her to muse in silence over what might have happened if he had stayed. Mickie was still very much a woman at war with herself. She wanted Matt very badly, but she also wanted to best him at his own game.

The soft clink of cutlery and filled wineglasses died down momentarily as Sarah Kehoe whisked away the nearly empty tureen of clam bisque and returned with a steaming platter of trout that she had caught just that afternoon. After Matt had left, Mickie had watched her from the bedroom window as she patiently chopped a hole in the shore ice and dropped her hooked lines into the dark water below. Within an hour she had caught two dozen fish.

There was a rippling murmur of delight as everyone caught the scent of the delicate orange sauce in which the trout had been poached.

"You certainly know how to throw a party, Matt," Mickie said, looking at him over the edge of her wineglass.

His eyes were soft and playful in the flickering candlelight. "I'm glad you appreciate my efforts."

Mickie smiled slightly, pleased at the course the evening was taking, in contrast to her disastrous and humiliating midday adventure. She hadn't missed the narrowed look that Sondra had cast in her direction as she took in Mickie's slim white pants and her simple but alluring bronze sweater, loosely woven and scooped low in the bodice. The unusual color and texture of the pullover were a lovely contrast to the coppery sheen of her hair.

Mickie had come into the dining room early, setting her tiny evening bag on the place mat to Matt's left. Sondra's dark eyes had flashed in annoyance when she had realized that she would be forced to share Matt's attentions with her rival.

Even though she had been conversing with Jerry on her right, Sondra hadn't missed the interchange between Matt and Mickie. She glanced over at Mickie with a deceptively sweet smile. "Have you recovered from your afternoon's misadventure?" she asked in a tone that was a subtle note louder than the other conversations going on around her. She took advantage of the attention she had drawn to herself by launching on a witty and caustic description of their encounter with Mickie on the front steps of the lodge. "Poor thing was a mess," she concluded. "I thought she'd decided to use herself as bait in the Kehoes's fishing hole."

Loud guffaws greeted this amusing thrust. Jerry was still laughing and shaking his head as he added his wit to the ribbing. "Boy, Mickie, that was a real *cheechako* stunt, getting caught under the eaves like that."

Mickie's gaze met Matt's inadvertently as both of them heard the lodge manager make his teasing observation. Touché, her expressive gray eyes seemed to tell him. Your friends are paying me back richly for the hazing my Kotzebue friends gave you.

His eyes crinkled in amused understanding at the subtle message her glance conveyed. Then she looked away from him and launched into a good-natured defense of herself. "Listen, you people. At least I ventured outside today rather than staying cooped up inside like a hibernating bear!" She laughed, her cheeks a healthy pink from exposure to the midday sun.

"While you were down there, did you happen to notice LaCrosse's old cabin?" Matt asked her.

"Yes. It was wonderful to see that the old place wasn't destroyed."

Matt turned to Sondra, who was listening to their conversation with a jealous ear. "Mickie was here at Spruce Lake years ago when it had nothing but the old trapper's cabin beside it."

Sondra's eyes were alert and as malignant as a snake's. "Oh, really? That was the *first* time until today?" she inquired, her gaze boring into Mickie's with a triumphant expression.

Mickie had the grace to blush at being caught out in her deception and for once had nothing to say in reply.

When the meal was over everyone made their way into the main room, where coffee and after-dinner liqueurs were to be served. After a while somebody turned on the stereo and the room was filled with lively, upbeat music. Sondra immediately claimed Matt, while Mickie found herself dancing with Larry Petersen. Song followed song and Mickie danced with every man in the room . . . except Matt. Sondra's monopoly was finally broken when Larry invited the designer onto the floor and there was no way she could refuse without appearing rude.

Mickie had wandered over to the pine bookshelves tucked into a corner near the bar and her eye was caught by a small, carved ivory figure. She took it from the shelf, running her fingers gently over the smooth surface; it had been sculpted in the form of a whiskered seal.

"You have a real tactile appreciation of art." Matt spoke behind her.

She whirled to face him. "I was just admiring this little guy. The craftsmanship is very familiar to me. The men on Little Diomede sculpt figures out of walrus tusks and so do a few of my friends on Russian Harbor. I had no idea you appreciated native art." The words were almost an accusation.

His eyes moved over her lightly. "There are a lot of things you don't know about me, Mickie."

She raised her chin, determined to meet his glance. "I'm sure there are, but—"

Her reply was cut off as Sondra drifted over to join them. "Matt, darling, be an angel and make me a whiskey and soda, will you?" She tossed her heavy hair over her shoulders. "I'm absolutely parched."

Mickie shrugged her shoulders and moved away toward the fireplace without waiting for him to excuse himself. She watched Matt and Sondra together at the bar, the way her hand lifted to brush his hair back from his forehead or to lightly caress his neck, and she remembered Jerry's curious words spoken earlier in the day: *Matt craves affection.*

She wondered how true that was as she recalled something else that Jerry had told her. Matt's mother had died when he was eight and the elder Greenslade had raised his sons alone—without a woman's help. Mickie wondered if Matt had built up an ideal vision of femininity in his mind that no real woman could touch.

Maybe that was why he had no women in his life now, except for Sondra's "friendship" and his business partnership with Mickie. She shook her head proudly, deciding then and there that she wouldn't allow herself to be boxed into one small corner of Matt's life. At times she had sensed his grudging respect for her abilities, but suddenly she found herself wanting more than that. She was curiously reluctant, however, to ask herself precisely what the "more" she wanted from him was.

Someone had dimmed the lights, so that the room lay in dusky shadows created by the flickering flames of the fire. A medley of slow tunes came through the speakers.

Mickie watched as Sondra took her drink from Matt and wandered over to speak to Jerry. Matt came round the bar and perched on the stool where Mickie had sat earlier in the day. The soft slumberous voice of a female vocalist filled the room and Mickie stood up, moving quickly—before her resolve could slip away—to stand before Matt. She cocked her head and held out her hands. "Would you care to dance?" she asked, a trifle breathless at the thought of her brash behavior.

His grin dissolved her fears. "I thought you'd never ask."

He stood up, long-limbed and graceful. She hesitated only a second before slipping her arms around his neck. They drifted off into the night shadows that hovered near the edges of the room. Matt leaned back to stare down at her, his brow lifting quizzically. "When I held you like this once before on a dance floor you became very annoyed with me."

Her eyes met his. "I hadn't learned yet what I like."

Matt tightened his arms around her, murmuring into her hair with a low laugh, "You catch on very quickly, Mickie."

She leaned her head for a moment against his shoulder, content to feel his slow, powerful pulse which was such a contrast to her own. They seemed made for one another as he twirled her around with slow, sensual grace. Mickie felt a surge of desire quiver through her, followed by a mixture of elation and confusion. My God, she asked herself, am I fooling him or myself?

The hypnotic mood was shattered as someone switched on the overhead lights and Ron Harris's brash voice called out, "All right now, enough of this romantic hanky-panky. We're going to get down to some real business now: five-card draw," he teased. "Matt, I've got to get back that fifty bucks you won off me three months ago."

Matt laughed and slowly drew apart from Mickie. "Interested in a little poker?"

She shook her head. "No, thanks. I may not be able to bluff as well as I thought I could. . . ."

Ron's voice rang out once more above Mickie's soft refusal. He was speaking to Sondra this time. "Are you in the game?"

Her eyes had been fixed intently on Matt and Mickie, but she shifted her gaze to Ron as he spoke. "Sure, I'll play," she said at last, lifting a thin cigarette to her lips and lighting it with slightly shaking fingers. Mickie quickly murmured "Good night" to Matt and left the room, Sondra's eyes following her every step of the way.

Mickie sat at the window in her dark room for a long time, staring out over the shadowed winter landscape. She thought deeply about Matt and her feelings for him. To her dismay she realized that her playacting and her real feelings were blurring together indistinguishably. She could no longer draw a dividing line between her desire to get even with him and her growing desire—which was beginning to eclipse everything else—to have him for her own.

After a while she realized that the muscles of her neck and shoulders had grown stiff. She remembered the redwood tub and impulsively went out into the corridor, heading toward the stairs.

She opened the door that led out to the deck and was relieved to see that no one else was there. The water was as dark and silent as the sky above. Mickie opened the closet door and glanced through the array of bathing suits that had been stocked there, finally choosing a bronze-hued crocheted bikini that appeared to be her size. Its color reminded her of the sweater she'd worn down to dinner.

She came out of the changing room, savoring the feel

of the warm, almost silken air against her bare limbs. She noticed a timer on the wall, so she flicked it to the "on" position. The water in the tub began to froth and bubble with a mysterious life of its own. Gently Mickie eased her tense form down into the hot, swirling pool which caressed her with pulsating jets of water. She laid her head back against the tub's edge, staring out into the cold, star-filled beauty of the night. Finally she closed her eyes and relaxed. "Matt was right," she whispered to herself. "This is utterly blissful."

She had lost track of how long she'd lain in the hot, pleasantly swirling water when a slight sound caught her attention and her eyes flickered open lazily. She gasped in wordless surprise as she stared up at the lean male outline towering above her.

"Hello, Mickie," Matt said slowly. "I hoped I'd find you up here."

She continued to stare, unable to keep her eyes off him. He was naked, except for a pair of navy trunks, and the only word for him was "magnificent." He slid down into the tub, immersing himself completely before resurfacing to stand beside her like a triumphant Neptune. Drops of water clung to the thick matted hairs of his chest and formed into warm rivulets which trickled down over his flat, hard stomach.

"What happened to your poker game?" she managed to ask at last.

"It was just a game. I got bored after a few hands." His eyes moved restlessly from Mickie's face to the starry black dome above their heads, then back to her again. "Well, what do you think of my luxurious 'toy,' as you called it?"

"I have to admit you were right." She laughed. "It's pure bliss."

"Did you know there's a light inside the tub, or are you just modest?" He grinned and reached to flick a switch that flooded the water with a soft, pearly incandescence.

Matt stared down at her curvaceous form, shimmering and magnified by the combined effects of the water and the light. "That color suits you," he told her. "I thought so earlier this evening and I think so now."

She glanced down in embarrassment at the tiny crocheted triangles which revealed far more than they hid. "You've got quite an imagination if you can envision a whole garment from this skimpy fabric," Mickie remarked with a trace of nervous laughter.

"I wasn't thinking of putting clothes on you," he teased in return. "More the opposite, as a matter of fact." His intimate words were electrifying.

He slid down into the water again and sat beside her on the submerged bench, his thigh lightly touching hers. "Better enjoy this while you can. We're flying out tomorrow."

She sat straighter, her shoulders coming out of the water. "Where to?" she asked, perplexed.

"Where do you think?" He laughed. "I want to buy a few more ivory carvings for the lodge; you mentioned the artisans on Russian Harbor."

Mickie half-turned toward him. She should have felt triumphant that—for the moment, at least—Matt was giving in to her. She had won, hadn't she? Then why did triumph taste so bitter? "Matt, I . . ." she began, reaching out to touch his cheek with her wet fingers in a tentative caress.

He caught her hand and pressed her palm to his lips, while with his tongue he licked the moisture from its surface in a teasing, extraordinarily sensual movement. Then he gently caught the skin between his teeth and shook it playfully, as if he were a cat teasing its prey.

A hot breath of excitement fired her soft laughter. "Matt," she whispered again, all other thoughts driven from her mind by the promise of what his lips and teeth and tongue might do to her, "you're wicked."

"Mickie," he growled, the low rumbling sound a blend

of laughter and passion, "you do bring out the beast in me."

He turned toward her and with his free hand reached out to explore upward over the rounded curve of her thighs and hips, the undulating pressure of his caress like liquid fire spreading its electric incandescence over her. He shifted once again, so that his long body was over hers, the swirling waters of the tub creating a pulsating cushion between them. Then he pulled himself up against her, their limbs sliding wetly against one another until Mickie thought she would explode in unbearably exquisite agony. His mouth found hers as he drove her head back against the tub's edge with the almost savage pressure of his kiss.

Matt's hands moved upward along her back, his fingers swiftly untying the strings of her top so that, to her dismay, she opened her eyes to find the tiny bit of crocheted fabric floating away. In that same instant the whirlpool timer clicked off so that the steamy, roiling water became still once again. Matt drew back a moment to stare down at her. Mickie's breasts, half-submerged below the still surface, were like round, pale globes, the nipples erect and pink with desire. With a sharp intake of breath he lowered his head again.

But before his lips could imprison her flesh with their possessive mastery Mickie turned swiftly and stood up. Matt reached out for her and she found her naked breasts pressed against his wet forearm. With his free hand he traced a light pattern down the bare, wet expanse of her back. "What is it?" he asked, his low tone not quite concealing the rough impatience he felt.

"Let me go, Matt!" she whispered in a strangled voice, beating down the aching wave of desire that still threatened to engulf her. "We've gone too far. Besides, how can you think of making love to one woman while another is waiting for you downstairs?"

He released her suddenly. "If she were my woman, do

you think I'd be up here now, Mickie? You're still at it, aren't you? When it suits your purposes you put me in the role of conniving villain because you'd rather deal with that simplistic image instead of a real live man."

She climbed out of the tub, her arm held protectively over her breasts, and picked up a large white velour towel from the bench. Despite the cozy softness that surrounded her as she wrapped the towel around her wet form, Mickie shivered slightly. "I know you're a 'real live man,'" she retorted. She had intended the words to be a taunt, but after she'd spoken them aloud they sounded curiously like a plea. "How could I help but know that after the way you . . . you held me just now?"

"Come back, Mickie," he said softly. "I'll show you the loving kind of man I can be."

She backed away. "I'm afraid, Matt." Her gray eyes were brooding yet hungry, caressing the bronzed width of his shoulders and his long, muscled torso that gleamed wetly as he pulled himself out of the tub.

"What are you afraid of?" he demanded huskily, coming toward her with his slow stride. "I just want to hold you, Mickie, to feel you in my arms. There's no use in our fighting that. We both know the attraction is too strong. It's inevitable."

A little gasp escaped her lips as his fingers closed around her upper arms and his mouth came down to feather her lips in a hungrily tender exploration.

"Touch me, Mickie," he growled. "Don't make me beg."

She thrilled to the power her womanliness held over him. Now the tables had turned and the strength and sense of control were hers. Yet the risks were still great, she knew, as his mouth moved down to taste the sweetness of her throat. She couldn't take without giving, and how she wanted to give—to taste the fulfillment he promised.

Mickie stood on tiptoe and pressed her lips to his

shoulder, savoring the salty moistness of his skin, the faint undertaste of musk and wool that clung to him.

"Touch me, Mickie," he commanded again, his impatience mounting. "Show me you're as much a captive of desire as I am." Need vibrated through his voice so that it rumbled low and husky, an animal cry.

Her fingers, warm and gentle, came up at his bidding to caress the sinewed shoulder with the same enticingly gentle boldness her lips had expressed. They whorled in soft circles of pleasurable exploration and ringed the hollow of his throat. His pulse drummed against her fingertips, a darkly passionate rhythm that drew her into the misty depths of fevered desire.

Mickie lifted her arms to encircle his neck, but as she did so the modestly wrapped towel slid away. Her naked breasts were crushed against the hard wall of his chest as Matt pulled her close and she gave herself up to sensual delight as her tender coral nipples were teased by the wiry mat of hair on his chest, to the cool glissando of Matt's fingers as they swept down the supple ridge of her backbone to cup her hips.

Those pleasure-giving hands were lifting her now and Mickie felt with delicious shock the pressure of his leg as he hooked it around hers, and they eased down to the tile floor in an intimate entwinement.

With his leg still tangled with hers, Matt drew back to look at her in the shadowed moonlight. His fingers moved in a lazy zigzag down her torso, stroking the pale gleam of her soft, full breasts and the shadowed hollow of her waist, the curve where her hip swelled in feminine promise.

His touch ignited a flame deep inside her and sent its warmth licking along her nerves.

Now the power had shifted and Matt was the conqueror, the dark thief plundering the secret cache of her womanliness. With a muffled cry she submitted helplessly as his strong legs pried a passageway along the soft curves of her inner thighs. He bent over her then and his lips trailed in the wake of his slow, sweet invasion.

"Mickie, you push me to the edge of ecstasy," he whispered, his breath feathering along her thighs. "I'm flying blind, love, lost in a white-hot storm of passion." Then he grazed her hipbone with his tongue, drinking in the warm, tantalizing musk of her own rising passion.

The soft rumble of his self-mocking laughter floated up to her in the shadowy darkness. "You've turned my world upside down, Mickie," he went on in the same husky, caressing voice, "until I'm not sure whether you're a devil or an angel."

Matt pulled himself up, planting a lingering kiss on each breast before lying beside her again. His passionate eyes searched hers until she was compelled to speak.

"I'm neither one nor the other, Matt," she whispered at last, tearing herself back from the sweet lassitude that threatened to lull her into forgetfulness.

His eyes raked her gently. "You've done something to me, Mickie, that no other woman has ever done. You've woven a spell; you're an enchantress."

She lowered her eyes to hide the pain in their depths. Matt was vulnerable now, but the triumph she should have felt wasn't there. "Enchantments only happen in fairy tales, Matt. This is real," she replied, her voice imbued with irony. She felt cheapened by the trickery she had meant to put into play: to use her feminine wiles to win concessions from him.

"Mickie, I want to make love to you," he murmured with a trace of his old impatience.

"No." She pulled herself up and groped for the towel which had fallen in the blind forgetfulness of her passion. "No, Matt," she whispered, her head turned away from him. "I'm more afraid of losing than ever."

Brushing her shoulder with his warm lips, Matt teased, "There are no losers in love, Mickie."

The words seared her and she suddenly wanted to

punish them both. "Not even for Sondra?" she flung at him softly.

That spurred Matt to anger. "Why the hell bring her up? She has nothing to do with you and me, Mickie."

She shook her head miserably. "I have to go, Matt. I'm tired of subterfuge, of games."

He eyed her narrowly, sensing that she was hiding something. "What do you mean?"

She wouldn't reply. She sensed that for Matt love was a game to be indulged in between his cutthroat dealings in the real world and she had entered into it willingly, hoping to beat him with his own cards. But she was no Sondra, content to be a part-time player. When Mickie gave herself to love she wanted it to be far more than just a game.

She got up hastily and Matt rose beside her. "Don't follow me," she whispered, her voice hard to mask the pain she felt. Then she turned and ran.

8

~cececececece~

Mickie slept later than usual the next morning. She was afraid to face Matt, afraid to face her own tumultuous feelings. She dressed and packed her bag slowly, wandering every so often to the window. Through the soaring pines she glimpsed the ice-covered lake and the faithful silver Cub waiting to ferry them to their next stop.

Matt had given in with such suddenness that it had left her off balance. Had he been teasing when he'd said that he wanted to return to the island in order to pick up more of the finely sculpted ivory work? Or had it indeed been the truth, spoken because he'd been won over by her seductive charade?

She had pretended to herself that the game would be an unpleasant one played against her will, but it had been a lie. From the very first moment she had loved her pretense of uncertain surrender until it became no longer a clever illusion but a true reflection of her feelings. So why hadn't she surrendered completely to him in the spa when her physical senses had screamed for it? She realized that she had been afraid of his strength of will, afraid of being diminished in some way by his power over her.

She slammed the suitcase shut. "I want him," she admitted aloud at last. She knew that he wanted her, too, but she would be damned if she would let herself become his casual mistress, waiting for the crumbs of affection he'd scatter her way, just as Sondra waited. A low gurgle of ironic laughter escaped her lips. Just a few days before she had been afraid that her womanly emotions were frozen and locked away, incapable of being touched. Now these same emotions threatened to wash over her in a flood tide that would send her recklessly into Matt's powerful arms. "Annie, dear," she murmured, laughing bitterly, "how right you were!"

When Mickie went downstairs a few minutes later the whole lower floor seemed deserted. She knew she had missed breakfast, but she hoped that Sarah Kehoe would have a pot of coffee still warm in the kitchen. Mickie wandered off uncertainly toward the lodge's service area. She walked past several empty offices and a small laundry room until she found the kitchen. The door swung inward soundlessly and she found herself in a narrow hallway bounded on both sides by pantry shelves. In the distance she heard running water and the faint clatter of dishes.

She was just about to take a step in that direction when her ears picked up the sound of feet approaching from the kitchen beyond. The long, heavy stride of a man was followed by the click of high heels on the tiles and an instant later Mickie heard Sondra's voice raised in a strident whisper. "Why won't you tell me?" she demanded. "You've slept with her, haven't you?"

Mickie held her breath as Matt's familiar low voice—his anger barely held in check—echoed in the room. "It's none of your damned business, Sondra. But, if you must know," he added with acid mockery. "we have shared a bed."

"I knew it! That little red-haired tease has wrapped you around her little finger," Sondra cried, her normally languorous voice shrill with venomous jealousy. "You're so damned blind . . . !"

Mickie's face drained of color. They were discussing her and she'd become an inadvertent eavesdropper. Horribly embarrassed and fearful of being discovered, she retreated on tiptoe through the swinging door before she could hear another word spoken between the quarreling couple.

Five minutes later Mickie was standing, anxious and restless, in the lodge entryway when she again heard the heavy tread of a man's boots. She turned to see Matt approaching, his arms laden with cases. Glancing up to meet his eyes as he came closer, she saw that they were hooded, revealing nothing. What on earth could have occurred between him and Sondra? she wondered.

"Let's get going, Mickie." The tight-lipped command was issued as he pushed open the front door with his boot.

She had no option but to follow him outside, grabbing her suitcase and slipping in the partially melted snow as she struggled to keep up with his rapid pace.

"You fly," he called over the wing to her as he loaded the luggage into the plane. His voice was as brittle and sharp-edged as the morning air.

Mickie was grateful that she had the familiar controls of her plane to occupy her attention as they lifted off from the lake surface and skimmed the vertical cliffs which bound Matt's lodge in its frozen, solitary setting. She hardly dared wonder how Matt might have responded to Sondra's vicious accusations. Had he admitted to a depth of feeling for Mickie that he could never feel for Sondra? Even as the hopeful possibility rose in her mind, Mickie knew that it couldn't be true. Matt's features had been grim and forbidding, imparting an even harsher quality than usual to the rough planes of his face. He had seemed to withdraw into himself, out of reach of both women.

Mickie flew steadily northwest, her clear eyes fixed straight ahead and her gloved fingers gripped tautly around the control lever. An hour later she breathed a little sigh of relief as Ugashik rose up out of the flat tundra. The old gold rush town was perched at a bend in the wide river that split the ice-swept northern plain. She brought the Cub down in altitude and dipped her wings by way of greeting before starting on the final approach to the snow and ice of the river.

As she brought the plane in Mickie noticed that several bundled-up forms had emerged from their homes of sod and peeled clapboard and were running toward the place where they knew the Cub would taxi to a stop. She was grateful for the friendly, silent welcome of the Eskimo villagers a few moments later. Their shy nods and smiles were infinitely preferable to the grim visage of the man beside her.

In the end they stayed on the ground for only a few hours, long enough to drink invigorating black coffee and to load up a large generator part which would have to be repaired in Nome. The villagers had been without electric power for more than a week, a fact which hadn't bothered them too much, since they had simply burrowed down more deeply into their sod embankment homes and lit kerosene lanterns. But the generator breakdown had forced the closure of the drafty clapboard school and the faces of the residents were wreathed in smiles as Mickie promised to do her best to get them a replacement before the month was out. They smiled even more happily as Matt brought out a case of canned milk and fruits that Mickie realized had been put together from his own well-stocked pantry at the lodge.

She regarded him with curious eyes, thoroughly perplexed by the seemingly conflicting sides of his nature. At least, she noticed with a trace of relief, he seemed to have relaxed somewhat from the taut edginess that had gripped him since they had left the lodge.

The curling drifts of smoke rising from Ugashik's wood stoves vanished in the crystalline air beneath the Cub's skis as they became airborne once again. After a while she turned to Matt. "Those villagers appreciated your gift," she observed quietly. "It was a very kind thing to do."

"Even a villain like me has his generous moments," he replied with light mockery.

"Please, Matt. I don't need you to remind me that I've behaved like a fool." She reached out and briefly touched the corded muscle of his outer thigh.

His eyes, deep and hard as aged oak, followed the movement of her hand. "I told you once before, Mickie, that I'd leave it up to you to decide what our relationship would be. Somehow, I don't think you've forgotten that." Then he turned away to gaze out the side window, his jaw resting meditatively on his suede-covered fist.

The rocky profile of Russian Harbor rose before them from the Bering Strait. Mickie noticed that in the short week since they'd flown to the island the shelf ice had already diminished a little more. The wintry fastness of the sea was breaking up into jagged chunks of ice, agleam in the sunlight like diamonds against crinkled, blue-gray satin. Within a few weeks, Mickie thought to herself, she'd be replacing the Cub's skis with wheels as brown earth replaced snow and ice on the Alaskan peninsula.

Mickie sighed as she made the familiar approach to the island. The transformations in the terrain below reminded her of the swift and unpredictable changes that had come over her. When they'd flown into Russian Harbor before, Mickie had been like a tigress jealously guarding her lair. This time she felt more like a vulnerable kitten. Matt Greenslade had beaten back her defenses until he had left her trembling with need. Now, without warning, he was again cold and aloof, locking Mickie out of his world. She guessed that the change had to do with the argument she'd overheard. Mickie wondered what more had been said between Matt and Sondra but, of course, she couldn't ask.

Ten minutes later they were inside the Navocks's cozy home, slipping out of their parkas and warming their hands before the blazing wood stove. Charlie shoved his stool back farther to make room for the newcomers, although he barely looked up from his work. He was engrossed in carving a small animal out of walrus tusk, using the traditional Eskimo spinning tool which he held with his teeth while the sharp-tipped end delicately incised the ivory. After a while he set aside his small sculpture and stared up at Matt. The two men regarded one another like wily adversaries, each waiting for his opponent to make the first move.

Matt seemed to relax after a few moments and he squatted down beside the stubborn old man. "How's your arm, Charlie?" he inquired gruffly. "Did you have a reaction to the shot?"

Charlie stripped several layers of clothing back until he revealed a length of scrawny but tensile shoulder and arm. "It swelled up a little, but that was all," he said proudly. "This old skin is tough. I'm ready for the next hunt as soon as walrus is spotted."

"And in the meantime you create your own," Matt replied, reaching out to pick up the half-formed ivory walrus that Charlie had set aside.

Mickie watched over his shoulder as Matt hefted the piece in his hand and ran his fingers over the simple lines that had the power to evoke such a strong sense of movement and life. The two men began to converse and Mickie moved away to join Nanny in the kitchen.

The round, beaming woman was pulling what looked to be miniature plucked chickens from a sealskin pouch, but Mickie knew they were dovekies, the small black birds the islanders hunted by the thousands each June.

The birds were stored in the pouches and buried beneath rocks to be dug up during the winter. The blubber within the sealskin not only preserved the bird meat but imparted a distinctive flavor to it.

"We're finishing up the last of our winter stash," Nanny explained as she worked. "Summer will be here soon and the men will be busy hunting the birds for the next winter."

"What's new in Russian Harbor since last week?" Mickie asked.

"Oh, you know, life goes on," the woman remarked softly. "Ellie Hevalek is having back pains and thinks her baby may come early; she's a little worried." Nanny patted her own beautifully swelling abdomen. "Have you convinced your friend yet that your flights to us are very important?" she asked, her round black eyes intent and serious.

Mickie sighed. "I think so. We're here now, aren't we?"

The soft-spoken Eskimo woman nodded her head in delight at this reasoning. She reached out and squeezed her friend's arm. "You're a good woman, Mickie."

She felt less delight at Nanny's words than she had thought she would. In the back of her mind there was a niggling feeling of guilt that she had achieved her success at the expense of an open and honest relationship with Matt Greenslade.

Her unsettling thoughts were interrupted as sixteen-year-old Janet hurried into the kitchen carrying little Sarah Jane in her arms.

"Mickie, Mickie," the toddler cried happily, holding out her arms.

She took Sarah Jane from Janet. "How are you, sweetie pie?" she asked, hugging the plump, rosy-cheeked girl.

Sarah Jane's response was to reach into the sleeve of her shirt and pull out the yellow sock puppet that Mickie had given her the week before. Mickie threw back her head and laughed. "Good grief! What happened to her?" she cried, her eyes taking in the bedraggled lump of wool with the bits of orange yarn that once had been perfectly formed curls.

Nanny laughed too. "That child! She insists that the doll never leave her side. She eats with it, sleeps with it, visits the neighbors with it. You can tell your Annie that her creation made a real hit with Sarah."

"That I will," Mickie replied, thinking to herself that Annie's delicate woolen creations had found more than one appreciative audience that week. Her thoughts roved again to Matt, who was still in the living room building a tenuous bond of friendship with surly, autocratic old Charlie.

"Did Mama tell you the good news?" Janet asked shyly, her black eyes glowing.

Mickie looked up from the bedraggled puppet. "No. What is it?"

Nanny was laughing. "Oh! I completely forgot to tell her."

Janet smiled. "It's just that Grandpa Charlie has agreed to let me go to Nome to visit the rural nurse program for myself to see if they'll accept me as a student."

"That's wonderful news!" Mickie cried. "Will you want to fly out with us?"

"Yes, if you'll let me. We've collected the seventy-five dollars for the flight."

"Listen, Janet," Mickie put in quickly. "We're returning to Nome anyway, so we won't charge you. If you get there and decide the program's not for you, then you can use that money to pay for the return flight. Otherwise, you're going to need it for books."

Janet's eyes beamed her thanks.

Mickie had intended to tell Matt about the agreement she had made with Janet, but in the confusion as the rest of the Navock family returned home, excited at finding visitors from the mainland, the matter was driven completely from her mind.

Dinner around the Eskimo table was a prolonged social affair, despite the simplicity of the food itself. Mickie managed to down a couple of the chewy little birds with their strongly fishy undertaste, taking gulps of coffee between each bite. She couldn't help contrasting this supper with the elegantly contrived meals at the lodge and she realized that Matt was thinking the same thing when he cast a wry, faintly amused glance across the table at her. It was the closest he had come all day to acknowledging shared feelings between them and Mickie felt absurdly grateful for the look. It made him seem less distant.

The remains of the dovekies were cleared away at last and great bowls of blueberries were set on the table. The family had collected the berries in the fall and preserved huge quantities of them in wooden kegs. A murmur of delight swept through the room as Nanny brought out one of the cans of milk that had been part of Matt's gift. When the milk was passed to her, Mickie dribbled a scant teaspoon over the fruit in her bowl so that there would be more of it to go around for the Navocks. She watched in amusement as Matt did the same.

After the last cup of coffee had been drunk Matt pushed himself away from the table. "Nanny, Jem, Charlie, that was a thoroughly enjoyable meal and I thank you. But we really have to be flying out."

Charlie fixed him with a gimlet eye. "You ain't going anywhere, man."

For a brief instant it seemed as if the old hostility would flare up again between the two men. Then Charlie clarified what had sounded suspiciously like an order. "You can't fly out because of the bad weather that's moving in. Why do you think I was inside carving today instead of out hunting walrus? My old bones sensed the change in the wind. I told everyone to stick close to shore and they know well enough to listen when my knees creak."

Mickie didn't miss the anger and impatience that had flared in Matt's eyes, only to be dampened just as swiftly. He grinned in mock defeat. "Even a *cheechako* like me knows enough to take warning when an old Eskimo's bones ache."

Mickie helped Nanny and Janet with the dishes, then sat before the stove with Sarah Jane, whispering a bedtime story to her. The men of the Navock family had disappeared, evidently busy with their evening chores, so Matt sat alone at the dining table, playing solitaire and idly whistling the slow melody that he and Mickie had danced to the night before.

She was about to get up from the fire and join him when Nanny entered from the kitchen with a plate of cookies, setting them down on the table with a beaming smile. One of the Navock boys came running in then, eagerly calling for Mickie to come outside and see the injured fox that he and his companions had found. She handed the sleepy Sarah Jane to her mother, then hurried out to join the excited boys on the rocky hill above the village.

The wind was blowing fiercely on the low ridge. From her vantage point Mickie noted that the visibility over the Strait was already close to zero. Charlie's old knees hadn't lied about the swift and devastating change in the Arctic weather. Mickie squatted down with the village boys to examine the bright-eyed little fox that had already had the benefit of some amateur veterinary treatment. His injured leg had been splinted and the boys had caught several field mice to feed him until he was strong enough to hunt for himself.

Finally, unable to stand any more of the lashing wind that carried with it stinging droplets of sleet and snow, Mickie hurried back to the warmth of the Navocks's cabin. As she paused on the storm porch to remove her jacket she happened to glance through the small windowpane in the door and saw Nanny and Matt, deep in conversation.

Moments later, her description of the sleet and cold and the boys with their fox was dampened somewhat as her eyes took in Matt's grim features. He was regarding her with a tight-lipped expression that unnerved her. He said nothing, however, and Mickie had no time to wonder about it, because the Navock household was bustling again. Tools and hunting equipment were being cleaned and set aside for the following day's work, while the younger children raced around collecting their pajamas and toys.

As blankets and furs were pulled out from the long wardrobe at the end of the room Nanny came to join Mickie before the stove. "I am sorry that we don't have enough room and blankets to accommodate you and Matthew. But our neighbors the Revaks are gone to the mainland, so you can use their cabin for the night." Then she handed Mickie a nightgown of exceedingly soft white wool.

"Please, Nanny. I don't need the gown. You've already been so hospitable. You needn't do more. I'll be quite fine in my jeans."

Nanny insisted politely. "Mickie, you've become a dear friend. I want you to wear it." She smiled a little. "It was part of my wedding trousseau."

Ten minutes later Mickie and Matt entered the Revaks's small sod bungalow, which was dug deep into the hillside. The interior, with its low ceiling and windowless walls, was small and cavelike, but it would protect them from the storm's onslaught. Mickie stared about her with great curiosity, realizing that the rude little shelter must have been one of the oldest on Russian Harbor.

Matt went immediately to the stove and began to stoke it with short lengths of wood, and within a very few minutes the room was warm, its corners filled with strange, flickering shadows. Mickie went to stand beside him at the stove, shaking out the gown which smelled of camphor and sweet pine. "Nanny loaned me this nightgown; I don't think she's ever worn it herself."

He glanced over at her, his eyes curiously hooded once again. "You'd better put it on," he remarked almost indifferently. "You'll get pneumonia if you try sleeping in those damp jeans."

Mickie found a small room by the kitchen and pulled off the clothes whose cold dampness had soaked down to her skin. She slipped the soft wool nightgown over her head, marveling at the delicate embroidery work along the row of buttons extending downward from the lace-edged collar. With her damp garments in hand she padded barefoot into the small central room and draped the clothes over the back of a chair to dry in front of the stove. She was innocently unaware that the light from the open stove front shone through the fine wool of her gown, outlining her naked form beneath in exquisite detail. Then she looked over to Matt and saw the desire in his eyes, smoldering like hot embers, ready to leap into golden flame.

She moved quickly out of the light and stared about her again. "I feel like a frontier woman in this place," she whispered laughingly, to cover her own confusion and nascent desire. "Sondra called me that yesterday—a frontier woman."

Matt had pulled his stool farther back from the stove and sat snapping lengths of kindling in his hands. "Did she?" he remarked at last. "She can be a very clever judge of people. She's often pointed out things in my business associates that I wouldn't have noticed on my own."

Mickie felt a prickle of jealousy at his words. "Let's not talk about her, Matt."

He looked up then and she saw that the desire that had

flickered a moment earlier in his eyes seemed to have been dampened in some indefinable way. "What *do* you want to talk about, Mickie?" His tone was cool, forbidding. "About us, maybe?"

"Matt, what's wrong?" she asked, feeling unsettled by the guarded, almost angry mood that had crept over him.

He looked up swiftly. The charming grin was there again, although the corners of his lips were twisted a little in a faintly mocking way. "What could be wrong, Mickie? Isn't this every man's dream, to find himself holed up in a cave with a beautiful and desirable woman?"

She glanced around nervously again, feeling a slight shiver of expectation and desire run up her spine. "I do feel like I've stepped back ten thousand years," she replied, her eyes moving from the shadowed corner, its bed piled high with animal furs, back to Matt.

He stood up, his harsh laughter reverberating against the stone and earthen walls. "This place does bring out a man's more primitive urges."

Mickie turned to watch him as he strode with easy grace to the stove and pulled off first his jacket, then his shirt. His wide shoulders gleamed like bronze in the red glow of the stove. She watched in helpless fascination as he bared his teeth in a cruel, mirthless grin and moved slowly toward her. "I'm a man, Mickie. And it's become quite apparent to me that you've learned to behave like a woman." The rough, hypnotic timbre of his voice had her almost mesmerized. "But I think there's one more lesson this man has to teach you."

In one swift, sure movement he swept her up into his bearlike embrace, his fingers digging into the warm nakedness of her hips and torso beneath the woolen gown as he carried her toward the bed.

9

～～～～～～～～

He dropped her onto the thick furs, then eased his own bare-chested form down beside her.

"Matt," she whispered, fear and excitement mingling in her voice. "I'm not ready to . . ."

His mouth smothered her weak protest in a deep, exploratory kiss. His hands moved down her throat to the lace collar of the gown, loosening button after button until he had exposed her breasts to the teasing, circular pressure of his fingertips. Then his mouth moved downward as well, his warm lips moving along a slow, sensual path that led into the sweet cleft between her breasts with its faint scent of dew and wild tundra herbs.

"Matt, please," she whispered, aching with a wild longing and desire, yet not quite able to forget his strange moodiness.

He lifted his dark head so that his eyes, with their hard, golden glints, bored into hers. "Please what?" he returned roughly.

"I . . . I don't want it this way," she whispered.

Matt lifted himself onto one elbow and regarded her for a long moment. "Cowardly little tigress," he murmured sardonically. "You were boasting to all the world what you could do. Now, in the heat of battle, you try to retreat." He reached up and negligently flicked a curl from her cheek with one finger. "This is the moment of truth, mountain cat." He reached down to the hem of the gown and ran his fingers lightly over her calf to the swelling roundness of her thigh. "You got your flights. Now I'm ready to collect the payment. That's how you meant to work it all along, isn't it?" His eyes glittered with anger. "You used me. You knew that I wanted you from the moment I held you on the dance floor in Lil's place. You knew it; you sensed the heat in my blood. And like the cool little manipulator you are, you meant to use it to your own advantage."

Tears sprang to her eyes. "I was a fool, Matt, but please don't mock me anymore. I've been punishing myself. I don't need you to do it, too."

His laughter was deceptively soft. "Do you expect my sympathy, Mickie?"

Her tears gave way to sudden anger. "No, damn it. I just want the chance for us to start over again."

"Too late, Mickie," he mocked, his eyes raking her. "This is one battle that you're going to lose—and I'm going to enjoy winning."

The gleam of passion in his eyes fueled an answering fire inside her, but all her old fighting instincts rose up in tandem with her desire. "You wouldn't dare," she informed him with icy hauteur.

"We want the same thing, Mickie, my love. But you wanted it on your terms." He paused. "Now the terms are all mine." His mouth swooped down to capture hers in a swift, hard kiss. "That seals the contract," he murmured roughly. "Now all that's left is for us to work out the form of payment."

Breathless from excitement, anger and even a little fear, Mickie watched Matt pull himself up to a sitting position. Slowly she did the same.

They eyed one another as warily as cats, her stormy gaze taking in his bare chest, his long, denim-clad legs crossed casually at the ankle, the expectant gleam in his whiskey-dark eyes. Then her gaze darted to the door, gauging the distance she would have to run.

"Don't even think it, Mickie," he taunted softly. "Let's just see how tough you are now."

Her back stiffened, ready for battle. Who did he think he was?

"Take off that gown, Mickie," he commanded in the same soft voice undercut with steel.

"Why you . . ."

"Take it off," he said slowly. "I want to savor every inch of you." She glared at him mutinously. "You'd better do it now if you don't want to return a torn scrap to Nanny in the morning."

Eyes gleaming with fury, Mickie turned away and pulled the gown up slowly over her head. Then she tossed it to the floor, where it lay like a drifted pile of snow in the charged heat of the bungalow.

"You're beautiful, Mickie," he whispered at her back. "You're more beautiful than any woman I've ever known." Against her will, she felt herself responding to the caressing languor of his voice and the yellow-hot glimmer of his eyes as they swept down her naked back. Slowly she turned to face him as he went on talking. "But you're a hellcat, Mickie, a devil with red curls. I don't know how I could ever have believed otherwise."

Desire licked at her as his eyes devoured the richness of her breasts, like snowy peaks in the firelight. "I never claimed to be an angel, Matt," she whispered, her expression faintly teasing.

"Neither did I." He laughed as he leaned back against the wall, his eyes never leaving her for a second. "Now undress me, Mickie."

Her startled eyes widening, she made no move to comply.

"I said undress me." His voice held the same hint of a veiled threat that could so excite and frighten her.

With provoking slowness she pulled off his boots and socks. Her fingers hesitated over the narrow brass buckle at his waist; then slowly she unfastened it. When she hesitated Matt reached down to assist her.

Mickie's eyes swept over the length of his nakedness— the male animal in his prime. Their closeness in the primitive surroundings impelled an atavistic longing deep inside her. It seemed that from time out of mind they had shared the hot intimacy of this moment. They belonged totally to one another.

"Make love to me, Mickie." He was still commanding, but the command was tempered with a new gentleness.

She lifted her gaze to his, the depths of her eyes shot through with passionate emotion. Gone was the pride, the clash of wills that had divided them from the start. For now it was forgotten.

A smile, at once tentative and giving, touched her lips in response to his command. "I—I don't know how."

His grin was teasing and faintly wicked. "Come here, then, and I'll show you," he replied as he pulled her down on top of him.

Their kiss was long and deep, passing boundaries they'd never even reached before. Gently Matt pulled her up until she was straddling his stomach. She trembled with delight at the sensual onslaught of his hands molding the creamy velvet of her breasts, of her thighs pressed to him in heated expectation.

Female instinct took over and with her arms braced on his chest, Mickie lifted her hips. Slowly she guided him into her womanly depths, a muted cry of ecstasy escaping her lips as they found the measure of one another in a dark, unhurried rhythm.

She moved in an enchanted circle of desire, the sweetly compelling rotation of her hips guiding Matt to a whole new world that they themselves had created. They rode in tandem through the dark, tapestried landscape of their passion. Mickie was mistress of this new domain, her every movement channeling the course of their desire. She was infinitely feminine, yet infinitely strong, and she reveled in her new awareness of herself . . . and of him.

Through the haze of passion she laughed at the thought that she could ever have believed this could happen against her will. How she'd hungered for his love, for the fulfillment of their union. Dear God, she loved him! But the words were swallowed in a breathless cry as ecstasy mounted in an ever-narrowing spiral that carried them to uncharted peaks. Their passion broke in a violent storm of such intensity that it engulfed them body and soul.

With a final shuddering sigh Mickie fell spent to his chest.

"Matt, I love you," she whispered, listening in wonder to the savage pounding of his heart against her ear.

"Don't spoil what we just shared, Mickie."

She lifted her head to regard him, her eyes darkening in confusion. "Spoil it? Matt, I said I loved you."

His mouth was a thin, hard line. "We're both free and clear now, Mickie. The debt's been paid and there's no winner, no loser. Don't try to pretend it was more than that."

Mickie sat up and regarded him with horror-stricken eyes. "You really believe that I gave myself to you as the final play in a silly game?"

"Since when did the rules change?" he muttered impatiently. "I was taken in once by you. It won't happen again."

"Stop it, Matt!" she cried. "You're so wrong about me."

"Am I?" His words bit into her painfully. "You boasted to Sondra, didn't you? She told me this morning that you were manipulating me, that you had told her we'd had our disagreements, but you could bring me around to your way of thinking. At the time I couldn't bring myself to believe it, because there were moments when I'd imagined that there was a deeper feeling growing between us."

"Matt, there was!" Mickie broke in. "There is!"

He ignored her outburst. "And all the while you've been behaving like a conniving little cat, trading your claws and childish temper tantrums for a seductive whimper—still determined to get your way and trying to control things. I see that you promised a free flight to Janet without even bothering to consult me."

"I meant to!" she cried, angrily defending herself. She wasn't quite able to bite back the sarcastic retort which flew to her lips. "You've become so much the generous soul lately that I knew you wouldn't object. Besides, you're guilty of the same kind of disregard for my feelings. How do you think I felt when you took Sondra up in the Cub? Fawning over her, catering to her every little whim!"

"I owe Sondra something," he retorted sharply, standing up. "But I don't owe you a thing. You've cheapened yourself, Mickie. It was apparent to me days ago that you're a good pilot and your flight service is solid. I knew there wasn't any need to cut out Russian Harbor from the schedule, but you were too blind to see my feelings. You had to cast me in the role of bad guy and use your charms against me."

Her eyes filled with tears. "Matt, I'll admit it started out as a challenge, an amusing little charade. And I despise myself for that." She paused, her lower lip trembling uncontrollably. "I love you. The playacting was over the night you held me in your arms in front of the fire in my bedroom. But I had to gather up the shreds of my pride around me—to pretend that you hadn't touched me so deeply."

He had put on his shirt and was buttoning it swiftly. "You hurt me, Mickie. At least with Sondra I knew where I stood. We were two of a kind. My mistake was in daring to hope you might be different." The bitter finality of his words was echoed in his frozen stare.

Through her own teary eyes she watched him as he pulled on his jacket and gathered up one of the blankets from the bed. "Where are you going?" she demanded.

"I'll sleep in the plane."

Then he was gone and Mickie fell back against the pillows as her rage and humiliation were drowned in a growing sense of loss. She fell asleep at last among the tear-soaked bedclothes.

Mickie was awakened early the next morning by a pair of hands insistently shaking her shoulders. She stared up through puffed and bleary eyes until she finally focused on the worried features of Janet Navock.

She sat up swiftly. "What is it, Janet? What's wrong?"

"Where is Mr. Greenslade?" The girl's tone was urgent.

"He's at the plane. What happened?"

"It's Ellie Hevalek," Janet called over her shoulder as she scrambled back toward the entrance of the bungalow. "Her baby is coming early!"

Mickie disentangled herself from the warm nest of furs and stood up, shaking her head to clear it of the last vestiges of grogginess. Within five minutes she had dressed and was in the Navock kitchen, taking huge gulps of the scalding black coffee that Nanny had been boiling on the stove.

A minute later Matt strode in, refusing Nanny's offer to pour him a cup. "Let's go, Mickie. I'm going to need your help."

"My help?" Astonished, she looked up from her coffee. "I don't know anything about delivering babies!"

His fingers tightened around her arm as he pulled her

up from the rickety old kitchen chair. "Come on. I don't have time to argue with you."

Mickie looked up at him over her shoulder as he propelled her at breakneck speed toward the front door. "Why don't you have Janet help you?" she asked, not willing to admit that she was more than a little apprehensive at being asked to assist.

"Because Janet is little more than a child herself. This requires a steady woman's hand."

"Then have Nanny help you. She's had six of her own," Mickie persisted, still trying to wriggle free of Matt's steely grip.

Matt paused at that and whirled her around to face him. "Use that sharp little brain of yours," he said bitingly. "Nanny's close to delivering a child of her own. What effect do you think it'll have on her if she has to witness a dangerous delivery?"

They were heading out the front door and down the gravelly village path. "Why do you say that?" Mickie asked worriedly.

"Because Janet's brief description of the woman's symptoms makes it sound like a breech birth. Hell!" he swore under his breath. "I had one lecture on breech deliveries sixteen years ago during my medic training."

Mickie stared up at him with eyes that were faintly red from the tears she'd shed the night before. "You'll do fine, Matt," she said softly. "I have confidence in you."

"*We'll* do fine," he retorted as he propelled her through the front door of the Hevalek cabin.

Frank Hevalek was crouched at his wife's bedside, his eyes and limbs paralyzed with fear. Matt gently ushered the stricken father-to-be out of the house, then turned like a general to bark out orders to Janet, who stood hovering uncertainly by the pregnant woman's shoulders. "Janet," he said crisply, "find clean towels and blankets. Mickie, I want you to help me while I have a look at Mrs. Hevalek."

The pregnant woman whimpered softly as Matt began his examination, but Mickie held her shoulders and whispered reassuring words to her. After a few minutes he took Mickie aside. "Worse than I thought. It's a footling breech." He sighed in frustration. "I can only touch one foot, and you can't deliver a breech that way."

"Can't you just pull on the leg, Matt?" she whispered.

"No. The loose leg can bend and block the birth canal."

For what seemed like an eternity Matt struggled to shift the infant's position in the womb. His jaw muscles strained and his face was wreathed in sweat. Mickie and Janet held Ellie's shoulders, gently admonishing her not to bear down until Matt ordered her to do so. Finally Mickie reached out with a dry towel and gently wiped away the perspiration that was dripping into Matt's eyes.

"There." He broke the silence finally with a quick, sharp gasp. "I can reach both feet."

Matt gave the order to push and the woman let out a soft, barely audible scream. Then—miraculously—Matt suddenly held the wet, slippery newborn in his arms, a triumphant grin spreading over his angular face. Janet scurried over with a blanket to swaddle the lustily bawling infant, while Matt held him up to the exhausted, relieved gaze of his mother. Then Matt glanced over at Mickie and for a brief moment their eyes held and shared the keen feeling of triumph and joy at having helped to bring the Eskimo baby into the world.

Frank Hevalek poked his head around the door, a beaming smile suffusing his weather-beaten features. "Congratulations, Frank!" Matt called to him. "You have a son."

The whole village gathered to celebrate the safe arrival of the Hevalek baby, nodding with approving smiles in Matt's direction. By the time a belated breakfast had been consumed and a series of toasts made with the island's home brew, the foul weather had cleared sufficiently for the Cub to risk a takeoff.

Mickie sat in the rear seat, while Janet Navock occupied the front position next to Matt. After their brief, shared moment of joy at the newborn's delivery he hadn't deigned to look at Mickie again and she was grateful that there was a third person in the plane. It would make the bitter silence between them less apparent. She stared at the back of Matt's head, her eyes roving over the strands of black hair edging his collar. She resisted the urge to reach forward and caress the thick, springy mass. If he could be unyielding and stubborn, then so could she. She wondered what thoughts were passing through his mind, wondered at how deeply she had hurt him. But he had refused to acknowledge the truth of her words: She loved him.

What right do I have to expect him to believe that now? she asked herself bitterly. I've done nothing but use him and fling insults.

How could he ever trust her? Mickie wondered miserably if he'd look for solace in Sondra's arms. The designer had made it quite plain that she wanted Matt in the same way she would want a major furniture piece to complete the effect she'd chosen to create. Though she might be coldly ambitious, Sondra hadn't tried to trick or deceive him.

Mickie cursed her own deviousness, her subterfuge and argumentative temperament. Yet how could she have known that she would fall in love with the man she'd meant to best?

She was called back from her troubling thoughts as Janet's excited voice rang out over the engine's drone. "Is that the mainland?" she asked.

The deep cloud cover had broken up along the Seward Peninsula, allowing an unimpeded view of the icebound coastline from its southwesterly tip to Cape

Prince of Wales in the North. Matt urged Janet to peer ahead to the rock called Sledge Island which was the landmark for Nome-bound fliers.

The girl turned in her seat to regard Mickie. "I'm looking forward to seeing your town."

Mickie managed a quick smile. "I hope you're not expecting high-rise buildings and trees and parks. If you are, you'll be disappointed. Nome is located between the ocean and the tundra, so in a way it's as lonely and isolated as Russian Harbor."

"But you're happy there?" Janet replied, her words more a statement than a question.

Mickie leaned back in her seat. "I suppose I am," she said, speaking half to herself. "It's the only life I've known."

Ten minutes later the Cub was circling the Nome airfield and Sam Lansing's buoyant voice was crackling over the radio, bidding a warm welcome home to the Double M bush line, which was what he'd decided to christen the service.

"Thanks, Sam." Matt's voice was crisp and laconic as he spoke into the radio. "But the Cub won't be home long. I'm taking her out again tonight to Spruce Lake."

Mickie stiffened as she heard his words. Was he so eager to get back to Sondra? she wondered jealously.

There was no time for idle jealousy or bitter self-recrimination once the plane touched down. Mickie hurried to the airport hangar to enlist Jim Iniak's help in unloading the generator part they had brought from Ugashik. Once Matt and Jim had loaded it into Mickie's Jeep, and Janet had been settled up front beside Mickie, Matt came around to the driver's side and casually laid his arm on the lowered window. "I'm refueling and flying out again within the hour," he informed her crisply.

"The lodge can't survive another day without you, is that it?" She couldn't keep the bitterness from her tone.

"I have unfinished business there." His hooded eyes revealed nothing.

She glared at him defiantly. "Where the Cub goes, I go. It's still forty percent mine."

"Suit yourself, Mickie." He shrugged, indifferent. "I see that your forty percent is still insisting on telling my sixty percent what to do." His words were a clear reminder that he was still the boss.

Without bothering to reply she shifted into first and the Jeep moved swiftly over the frozen runway. As they drove through town Mickie pointed out one landmark after another to the wide-eyed Russian Harbor girl. They stopped at a machine shop just long enough to have the generator piece carted inside, then drove on down Front Street toward Mickie's home.

"You're more than welcome to stay here," Mickie said as she drove up into the long driveway. "Annie will enjoy your company."

Almost as if she had heard her name spoken, the old Eskimo woman appeared on the porch outside her cottage with a bundle of knitting in her arms.

After Annie had ushered the young girl to the guest room she returned downstairs and fixed Mickie with an accusing eye over the small breakfast table. "Well, you've been avoiding me ever since your little dinner party. I have a feeling something's going on."

"Annie, I don't have time to argue," Mickie answered as she folded hastily grabbed sweaters and underclothes and arranged them in her bag. "Besides . . . you were right. I've gotten in way over my head."

The old woman laughed gleefully. "You've fallen in love with him, haven't you? So why are you looking so miserable?"

"Oh, Annie, he despises me! He saw through my little ploy to save the Russian Harbor flights and now he thinks I'm a cheap phony."

"Never mind," Annie clucked. "That's just his man's pride complaining. It'll blow over."

"It's not that simple," Mickie retorted. "There's another woman involved—he'll see her tonight at the lake."

"What's she like?" the old woman asked curiously.

"Beautiful . . . and she wants Matt."

"Is he in love with her?" Annie sounded like a prosecuting attorney.

"No . . . I don't know," Mickie replied, confused.

Their conversation was interrupted as Janet came into the kitchen from the hall.

"I've got to take off, Annie," Mickie said, giving the old woman a quick hug and brushing her lips against the brown, wrinkled cheeks. "Bye, Janet! Good luck at the hospital."

Annie stomped over to the back door and called out to Mickie as she climbed into the Jeep. "Don't do anything rash, girl. This is no time for your stubbornness and hot temper!"

The two-hour flight to Spruce Lake was completed in a cold and stony silence that neither of them attempted to break. Matt brought the Cub down just as the sun was dipping below the horizon at their backs. Through the trees the windows of the lodge resembled long rectangles of yellow cellophane, bright with a warmth and cheer that seemed alien to Mickie's frozen, miserable heart.

Once they got inside they were greeted with jovial shouts from the lodge-bound group. Sondra, however, was glaringly absent. She appeared a few minutes later on the stairway, clad in a flowing caftan of cherry silk.

When the other woman came closer Mickie saw that her dark eyes were as watchful as a cat's as she attempted to assess the change, if any, in Matt's relationship with Mickie. What she sensed must have pleased her, because she visibly relaxed, then smiled as she ran forward to link her arm through Matt's. "Welcome home, darling," she said in her languorous voice. "We missed you."

Mickie carried her bag up to the room she'd occupied before. When she came downstairs again she was still clad in jeans, but had changed into the heathery-gray sweater she'd worn when she and Matt had first met in her office. The gray and mauve scarf around her throat picked up the tint of her somber eyes. She had done with her coquettish playacting.

As she approached the main hall Mickie heard the distinct throaty peal of Sondra's laughter. "I hope you don't mind the informality of the meal, darling," she was saying, "but Ron insisted that we all listen to the baseball game over the shortwave."

Matt's rough laughter cut into her apology. "Hamburgers and potato salad sound terrific, especially after the intriguing dinner I had with an Eskimo family last night." He described the meal of dovekies to his fascinated audience.

Mickie stepped into the room and, when the laughter at Matt's story finally died down, cocked her head and said clearly, "Did Matt tell all of you that he's made himself a hero in Russian Harbor?"

As eager demands for an explanation rang out Sondra whirled to glare at Mickie, who stood in the doorway with her arms crossed casually in front of her. Sondra's eyes seemed to narrow in speculation as she wondered what experiences the couple might have shared, but she turned around swiftly again when Matt began to speak. "All I did was deliver a baby."

Mickie came into the room and perched on the back of the sofa, not taking her eyes from Matt's face. "It was a difficult breech delivery—the woman and her son might have died otherwise," she elaborated.

Matt's eyes flickered over her, the muscles tensing along his wide jaw. Mickie returned his gaze steadily to let him know that she'd seen through his façade just as he had seen through hers. She guessed that he put on the role of cold cynic because that was what the rest of the world expected of him. But Mickie was certain that beneath that tough façade he was a generous and caring man. At least, she wanted to believe that. "Why so modest all of a sudden, Greenslade?" she goaded softly.

Her half-teasing gibe was swallowed up as the others clamored for this new story to be told. Matt had no choice but to launch into a description of the isolated village and the difficult delivery.

"Say, Matt," Ron Harris put in suddenly, "did they name the baby after you?"

Mickie smiled; the thought hadn't occurred to her before. Glancing over at Matt, she saw that it was an amusing idea to him as well. For a brief instant his eyes darted toward her with a laughing, questioning look, but just as quickly he shuttered their expression.

She was hurt by his turning away from her, even though she knew that she probably deserved it.

Ron turned to get her opinion. "What do you think, Mickie?"

She tried to smile. "I'm sure there's a good chance that a young Matthew Greenslade Hevalek will grow to manhood in Russian Harbor."

Loud guffaws of humor and delight greeted this answer.

Mickie barely picked at the food she had taken from the picnic-style buffet arranged on the bar. She sat at one of the low game tables and stared into the darkness as the baseball game blared from the radio. She tried not to notice Matt and Sondra as they sat talking quietly together before the fire.

Between innings Ron Harris sauntered over to join her. "Isn't this the life, Mickie? All the majesty of the wilderness and all the comforts of home," he teased, gesturing toward the shortwave radio with the beer in his hand.

"Ron, you're incorrigible," she replied in teasing reproach, grateful for the distraction he provided. "I'll bet there are some ice skates or cross-country skis lying around. We could all go for a moonlight trek."

He eased into the club chair beside her, his tanned, boyish features fixed in an expression of mock horror. "Are you crazy? It must be thirty below out there. If Matt wanted to be a real host to his California buddies, he'd put in a racquetball court."

"I know one Eskimo sport that might appeal to you, Ron. It's called the blanket toss." Mickie laughed, some imp of devilry making her words sound flirtatious and vaguely seductive.

Ron's blue eyes studied her carefully. "A toss in the blankets sounds very promising, Mickie. As a matter of fact, I have just the thing in my room." He took her hand and tried to pull her to her feet, his baseball game forgotten.

Laughingly she made him sit down again, the same mischievous imp keeping her from withdrawing her hand from his. "Aren't you at least going to let me explain what the game is?"

"Go ahead." He smiled. "I have a feeling there's a catch here."

She laughed again. "It's very simple. The Eskimos gather in a circle and hold the edges of a blanket while someone climbs onto it. Then they toss the person as high as they can—like on a trampoline. It's just a sport now, but in the past it was important to their survival because the person who was being tossed into the air had a quick view out to sea. It was a way of spotting whales." She paused, her gray eyes still teasing. "Now would you like to try it, Ron?"

It was his turn to sound reproachful. "Mickie, I thought you had something else entirely in mind," he told her as he caressed her hand with a light pressure.

Their tête-à-tête was interrupted as Matt sauntered over to their table, his eyes flickering disinterestedly over their joined hands. "Sorry I'm such a poor host this evening, but I'm tired. I think I'll take a dip in the tub before turning in."

Ron smiled up at his friend. "The rigors of childbirth too much for you today?"

Matt's lips twisted in a crooked grin as he shrugged. "It was a hell of a trick to play on an unsuspecting man." His sardonic words were as sharp as a double-edged razor blade.

Mickie's gray eyes, somber once more, flashed up at him, but he'd already turned on his heel and was walking away from them. Beyond his retreating back Mickie couldn't help noticing Sondra, who stood in the hallway shadows, undoubtedly waiting to accompany Matt upstairs.

Mickie tried to snuff out the image rising in her mind of Matt and Sondra together in the intimate glass-enclosed room with its steamy tub. A vivid memory leaped unbidden to her mind of the way her own limbs had moved against his, the way her heart had throbbed in a deep and urgent rhythm that was at once softened and heightened by the caressing jets of water. She felt a growing sense of sweet longing and bitter loss, but with a will she quelled the anguished emotions. Matt had made his choice, she told herself at last.

Her thoughts were called back to reality by Ron Harris's brash, happy voice. Only momentarily let down by Mickie's gentle rebuff, he was full of energy and plans once more. "How about joining us in a game of poker, Mickie?" he asked enthusiastically. "We'll just play penny ante."

"Why not go for high stakes?" she retorted, attempting to resume a playful air once more.

Ron whistled softly. "You must be some hot player, Mickie."

She leaned her elbows on the table and crossed her arms in front of her. "No, I'm not. In fact, I seem to have been on a losing streak lately. But go ahead and deal me in. After all, what do I have to lose?" She shrugged and her laugh was tinged with bitterness. "Matt already has my plane and my business."

Ron grinned as he beckoned Jerry Link and Larry Petersen to join them around the table. "Now *those* would be interesting stakes to play for," he conceded with a laugh. "Wish we could get Matt back down here to join us."

Again and again, as the cards were dealt and chips were tossed into the center of the table, Mickie's glance roved toward the hallway. But neither Matt nor Sondra reappeared downstairs.

Despite the others' choking cigarette smoke and her own stiff back Mickie stayed at the game with her three bantering companions until far into the night. She was unwilling to go up to the lonely solitude of her room to face her anguished, jealous thoughts.

But the game broke up at last and Mickie found herself climbing the stairs side by side with Ron Harris, his high spirits undiminished by the lateness of the hour. At the top of the stairway they stopped for a minute.

"Well, Mickie, you're a hot little player," he teased. "We'll have to raise the stakes for you next time."

"No! I was only joking," she retorted. "It's actually very painful for me when I lose."

"What! A thick-skinned Alaskan like you?"

A telltale hint of sadness touched her eyes. "That's only a surface illusion, Ron. Well, good night and thanks for the diversion."

"It's a pity I couldn't have provided more of one." He leaned down and kissed her lightly. "Good night."

Mickie made her way slowly down the corridor toward her own room. Her hand was on the brass doorknob when a sound caught her attention. She turned to face Matt as he padded slowly down the stairs from the tub room toward her. He wore nothing but a brown velour towel slung low over his hips.

She gasped inwardly, overcome by his taut aura of sexuality. As he approached, Mickie was reminded of a lean and hungry predator who had been waiting with ill-concealed impatience for his prey. The faintly menacing gold gleam in his eyes sent a thrill of subtle fear and excitement down her spine. "What do you want, Matt?" she demanded softly.

He leaned against the doorframe and crossed his arms over his dark chest. "You amaze me, Mickie," he whispered, his partially hooded eyes flicking over her with lazy disdain. "I'm in awe of the way you slide from game to game with such clever ease."

"Matt, you told me once that I was a coward because I preferred to deal with you as an ogre rather than a man," she told him in a low, angry voice. "Now it seems you're guilty of the same thing." She took a step closer to him, her chin raised stubbornly and her eyes flashing with pride. "I may have made a few mistakes, but I'm only a woman, Matt, no more and no less."

His eyes played over her. "I know that, Mickie." He paused before adding insolently, "and I suppose Ron Harris has been made intimately aware of that fact as well."

Her hand shot upward, connecting with his face in a satisfyingly sharp slap. She stared at the white imprint of her fingers against his cheek, their outline slowly deepening to an angry dark red. "Go on back up to your Sondra," she whispered bitterly, her breath torn from her in short gasps of outrage. "We have nothing more to say to one another."

With eyes half-blinded by tears she rushed into her room and tried to bolt the door. But Matt was too quick for her.

"How dare you follow me!" she cried, her tears supplanted by outrage as he kicked the door shut with his bare foot. "This is my room."

"Yes, but it's my property," he countered with a deceptive air of ease.

"That's just the way you think, isn't it?" she sniped. "You think your wealth can buy you anything!"

"It hasn't bought you." He came toward her lazily in the darkness.

"You're damned right it hasn't!" she swore with an air of bravado that was belied by her slow retreat in the face of his advance. "Why don't you take your money where it's appreciated? You and Sondra are the perfect pair. You regard women as nothing but objects to have around when it suits your fancy and she looks on men as pieces to fit into her personal designs."

"You self-righteous little idiot." Matt's eyes raked her coolly. "You're the one who's been toying with people's feelings. Take a look in the mirror, Kilpatrick, before you start up with your accusations. I'm getting tired of them. Why don't you grow up?"

"What is this, Matt?" she snapped sarcastically even as she continued to retreat before him. "A prelude to another of your lessons in showing me how to act like a woman?"

"That's not a bad idea at all, Mickie. You have a bad habit of not finishing what you start." His low laughter sent a little shiver along her spine and she realized that she'd been backed up against the window.

As they stood facing one another the bedside lamp flickered and went out.

"More of your intimidation tactics?" she asked, her lower lip trembling.

"What's the matter, Mickie?" he countered, laughing softly as his hands came up to rest on the cold glass to either side of her. "Afraid of the dark?"

"I'll scream if you touch me, Matt Greenslade," she whispered fiercely.

"You've used that threat before, Mickie." His words were a silken taunt. "It didn't work then and it won't now."

"Oh, really?" Her eyes glittered with rage as she took a deep breath and opened her mouth. But her brave challenge was destined to fail as Matt's hand came up swiftly to close on her chin while his mouth crushed down on hers to swallow her cry of defiance.

He took advantage of her parted lips to probe the velvet recesses of her mouth with a thoroughly intimate kiss that left her trembling. Against her will she found herself returning the searing pressure of his lips, kiss for kiss, until she felt that she might drown in the exquisite, brandied warmth of his mouth.

Then she felt him drawing away, leaving her breathless and desperately in want of more. When her eyes fluttered open at last Mickie saw that he was grinning down at her. "Any more tricks up your sleeve, Kilpatrick?" he demanded softly.

Before she could reply there was a quick rap at the door and she brushed past him to answer it. Jerry Link stood in the hallway. "Sorry to bother you, Mickie, but have you seen Matt around? The generator has gone out and I need his okay to go to back-up power tonight."

"I'm right here, Jerry." Matt's low, unruffled voice sounded at her back. "Shall we go take a look at the problem?"

Mickie watched them move down the shadowed corridor, then gently closed the door.

With a sigh she sank down into the easy chair before

the window and drew her legs up snugly beneath her. As her thoughts whirled she watched the moon rise above the mountain peaks to bathe the lake and woods in a cold, silvery light.

Matt had gotten his revenge for her subterfuge in an unexpected way—by showing her how vulnerable she was to him. Taming her was just another of the challenges in his life, she reflected in annoyance.

He had punished her all day with his cold withdrawal, while she'd used Ron to try and make him jealous. The two of them had set their own rules for this silly, hurtful game that was driving them farther apart. Why did they have such a need to inflict pain on one another? For herself, at least, Mickie supposed it was a means of self-protection. She was afraid of her own vulnerability, of the depths of her caring. It seemed like months rather than days since Matt had walked into her life as if he belonged there, and she realized with a sense of shock that she had difficulty in thinking of it any other way.

She hadn't wanted to face the truth, that she was tired of the demanding, lonely life she led. Annie's almost comical harping that Mickie find a husband for herself was her way of confronting the girl with a basic truth: Sharing your life with someone you loved was what made it worthwhile. But it had been easier and less emotionally risky for Mickie to go on the way she had been . . . until Matt. He'd brought a spark, a new sense of excitement, to her work and to her life as well.

Mickie had tried so hard to follow her father's dictums, but in doing so she'd shut off a part of herself. It was Matt who'd awakened all that, she realized, perhaps too late. In so many ways they were alike! Matt, too, had been compelled to become self-reliant, to depend only on himself, unwilling to trust anyone's feelings but his own. And Mickie had to face the unpleasant truth that her all-too-clever maneuvering had forced him back into his aloof shell.

Mickie blinked in surprise a moment later as the room was flooded with light from the bedside lamp. She stood up and ran nervous fingers through her tousled curls, knowing that it was all up to her now.

No longer was she a part of the cold darkness beyond the window. The woman within was warm with the need to give and to share. She had to try again to reach Matt, to make him understand the truth. For her, at least, the game had ended days before. She loved and needed him in a way she'd never known before. The risk of being hurt again still existed, but she had to confront him. She had to know what he wanted from her.

With tender eagerness she hurried out into the hall and toward his room. She stopped in front of the door and was about to knock when she heard the low murmur of voices beyond—one of them unmistakably feminine.

Mickie caught her breath to stifle the cry of pain that rose in her throat. How could she have been so naive? She had been ready to confess her love, but he'd put her from his mind the moment he left her room. It was all too apparent what Matt wanted—and it had nothing to do with a lifetime of loving and sharing.

If Sondra could be satisfied with that, then more power to her. But Mickie knew that as far as she was concerned there was no option left. She had to get away before she was hurt even more. But how? Angry and disillusioned as she was, Mickie wouldn't dream of stealing the Cub. She had relinquished her control of the plane the moment she'd signed her name to the contract. She had already given Matt enough reasons to distrust her; she wouldn't give him another.

Outside the moon rose higher in the black sky above the pines and almost as if on cue she heard the sled dogs in the pen, their howls rising in a wild and melancholy cry. Suddenly it was clear to her what she had to do.

10

The predawn air outside the lodge was as sharp as broken glass. All the moisture had been frozen out of it to coat the eaves of the building and the drooping pine branches with frost. Mickie's boots crunched over the snow as she ran down the moonlit path toward the old trapper's cabin.

The dogs howled joyfully when she pushed open the gate to their pen and she shushed them as best she could while she hitched them up to their sled. Ten minutes later the eight animals and their new mistress were swiftly skimming across the purple-shadowed snow. Mickie's eyes picked out the trail that Bob Kehoe had pointed out to her a few days before and she guided the straining animals in the direction of Lalak. She had no clear thought other than her overpowering desire to escape.

The winter landscape, so barren and dark, mirrored Mickie's own feelings. She told herself that she would be free again, but the words were miserably hollow. With unbidden clarity she realized that she wasn't running toward anything—she was running away.

Her mind reeled with feverish thoughts as she tried futilely to imagine how she would fill the void in her life.

She imagined herself selling the house in Nome and moving to Anchorage, finding an undemanding government job that would provide her with numbing security.

She had to forget Matt, to wall off the part of her heart that had been so deeply hurt. Then, although she thought she'd mastered them, the stinging tears began to flow again, only to harden and freeze against her lashes. Her heart had frozen in just that way; she despaired of ever feeling again.

Mickie realized that she'd been so busy worrying about the lives of her Russian Harbor friends that she had forgotten her own needs and been false to herself. She wasn't a game player and never would be. That was why Matt's accusations had hurt her so. He'd been all too ready to believe the worst.

Again she pictured him in her mind, stubborn and strong-willed, and a bitter little laugh escaped her lips. She'd probably built it all up in her imagination anyway —Matt wasn't the type of man who wanted commitment. Everything Mickie herself had been—proud, self-possessed, in control—he had matched and surpassed in his own personality. He hadn't denied it when she'd accused him of wanting a woman only when it suited his fancy.

She knew now that it was best that she had left. Having to face him again when she knew all this could only mean more heartbreak.

As Mickie was rehearsing the words she would say to the startled residents of Lalak when she arrived with the lodge's sled team her ears picked up a distant muffled sound, like the droning of a gnat. She risked a glance over her shoulder and her eyes picked out the familiar profile of the Cub, barely visible against the pale gray of the dawning morning.

She turned forward again and flicked the whip, her only remaining hope that she could reach the outskirts of the Eskimo village before Matt could overtake her in the plane. But it wasn't meant to be.

Moments after she had heard the distant warning drone the plane was directly overhead and she risked another glance upward to see it circling in a slow, lazy descent. It touched down on the snowy earth in front of her.

She drew the dogs to a halt and warily observed Matt as he climbed down over the wing and approached her across the snow.

He regarded her for a long moment, his eyes as clear and sharp as the frost coating the Cub's wings. "This is a fine return for my hospitality," he said at last. "I wake up to find you've stolen my dog team."

"You have my plane," she retorted, defiant still. "Besides, I wasn't stealing your sled. I was borrowing it."

He came up to her and cocked his head curiously. "Why?"

"I wanted to go to Lalak. I couldn't bear the atmosphere of the lodge any longer," she said, all her pride intact as she stepped back from the sled. "Now, please get out of my life—fly out of it forever."

"You're a fool if you think you can run away from me, Mickie." He held his mouth in a grim, tight line.

"You can't force me to go back with you!" she shouted as he came closer still and gently pried the whip out of her hand. A moment later he turned the sled around and with a flick of the whip sent the dogs racing back to the lodge.

Mickie turned, too, and ran blindly over the snow, but within two long strides he had overtaken her. Matt picked her up and carried her, protesting, back to the waiting plane. He climbed up onto the wing and dropped her into the passenger seat. "You always have to be the one in control, don't you, Mickie?" he accused as he snapped the safety harness across her lap.

Mickie regarded him stonily as he eased into place behind the instrument panel. "I'm not going back to Spruce Lodge," she informed him.

"Quit fighting me, for God's sake!" Matt rasped in irritation.

"What choice do I have?" she shouted over the whine of the engine as Matt pulled back on the control stick and the Cub lifted skyward. "I'm afraid not to fight you. I'm afraid of being swallowed up." The words came tumbling out helter-skelter, an echo of the churning thoughts that had harried her all night. "I understand now that the world is just one big challenge to you, Matt, and I just happened to get in the way. Your lifelong clash of wills with your father has spilled over and is poisoning everything else. It's made you hardheaded and made winning everything. It's made you . . . so damned cold." Her voice caught in her throat then and he glanced over at her swiftly. But she looked away, her eyes taking in the new course he'd set. "Where are you taking me, Matt?" she demanded.

"Someplace where we can talk—without interruption," he told her quietly.

"Talk about what?" she flung back, but he stared straight ahead as if she hadn't spoken.

They flew on in silence toward twin mountains that were split by a wide, snowy valley. Mickie's eye caught the blinding flash of sunlight where it reflected off something below.

As Matt brought the plane down in a slow descent between the two peaks Mickie glimpsed a small structure.

"What's that?" she asked in astonishment as her gaze took in the unexpected sight of the cantilevered hut rising like an angular sculpture from the upper reaches of the valley.

"My overnight hunting lodge," he explained tersely.

"I thought you didn't hunt anymore," she accused.

Matt glanced over at her again and something in his gaze sent a little shiver up her spine. "Going after certain prey still excites me."

Her eyes were somber and she wondered if he was toying with her again, if his need for revenge hadn't been quite sated.

The lodge was a rustic retreat, with only the essentials: a fireplace surrounded by thick rugs and a few easy chairs. Her eyes followed Matt as he tossed his jacket into a corner before crossing to the fireplace and hefting a pair of split logs onto the grate. She remained where she was by the door, half-ready to run back to the haven of the Cub. "Why did you bring me here?" she demanded finally.

He glanced across the room at her, his golden eyes mocking. "So you can scream to your heart's content, and try any other tactic you have a mind to."

"Why should I scream, Matt?" she mocked in return.

He grinned. "You've been kidnapped, haven't you?"

"I could still run." Her eyes flashed with defiance.

"You know I'd come after you, Mickie." He tossed a match into the grate, then went to stand before the window.

There was a certain inevitability to his words, an implied sense of possession that sent the blood rushing to her temples. "Why?" she repeated, hearing the word reverberate crazily in her brain.

For a long while Matt continued to stare out over the white, frozen valley, as if she hadn't spoken. Then he turned and came toward her, exuding a power and vitality that she responded to instinctively. "I think you know the answer to that, too," he replied, his voice rough with impatience.

But she shook her head in denial. "No, I don't," she whispered, feeling curiously weak as his hunter's eyes pinned her. "Tell me."

A low sigh of frustration and pent-up emotion escaped his lips. "I came after you because I had to know where the pretense ends and the real you begins, Mickie."

Her lower lip trembled uncertainly. "Damn it, I've tried opening up to you, Matt. But we both have such hard shells."

"We aren't talking about me," he growled.

"Oh, yes, we are!" Her chin shot upward with the old, reckless defiance. "You're afraid of commitment. You were willing to hang on to your relationship with Sondra long after it died, because it was safe and you wouldn't have to feel. I'll admit I ran away this morning because of her, but the ironic thing is I'm not jealous anymore. Sondra doesn't have an emotional hold on you. It's just that as long as she's in your life you don't have to run the risk of facing the real thing." With a shock, Mickie realized that she was crying.

"We're both alike, Mickie." His laughter was almost angry. "Both too clever by miles. You gave me just what I deserved. I don't blame you for walking out of my life." He turned away then and moved toward the door. "I guess that says it all."

"Not quite," Mickie retorted softly. "I just want you to know one thing. I meant what I said to you that night in the Revaks's bungalow." There was no quaver in her voice, no hesitation. "I loved you, Matt. There was never any pretense about that." She saw the flicker of uncertainty in the harsh, composed mask of his face. "Didn't you hear what I said?" She came forward, tears splashing from her eyes, until she stood directly before him.

Slowly his hands came up and his thumbs brushed the wet streaks that ran into the corners of her lips. Then his fingers were tracing the soft contours of her mouth. "I'm scared as hell that you can see so deeply inside me," he admitted at last, his voice pitched low. "And I'm scared of what I'm feeling now."

"Coward." Mickie laughed up at him shakily. "Then you should never have come after me."

His grin was rueful, teasing. "I had to, Mickie. It was a compulsion. You created a hunger in me I've never felt before."

The words were an echo of what was in her own heart, and as she reached up to twine her arms about his neck, Matt swooped her up into his arms. He laid her down gently on the rug in front of the fire, his hands reaching up to unfasten the top button on her blouse. "Besides," he teased, "turnabout is fair play. You gave me a lesson in loving that night in the Revaks's bungalow. Now I think I owe you one."

Her shadowed gray eyes laughed up at him. "Are you still intent on punishing me, Matt?"

Her question was swallowed up by his kiss, deep and unhurried, a kiss that blocked out everything but that moment. "If this is what you call punishment," he whispered as the rest of the buttons were swiftly undone and his hand slid beneath the silk to caress her breast, "then I intend to go on punishing you for the rest of your life."

Slowly they undressed one another, eyes and hands exploring with the same tender, unhurried ease. The firelight caught the shadowed clefts and rounded peaks of Mickie's satiny flesh. With his fingers Matt traced the flickering shadows along her thigh and the swelling curve of her hip until she wanted to cry out with pleasure. Then he was poised above her and she felt the hard length of him against her, welcomed the tantalizing grazing of his dark-matted chest against the rosy tips of her breasts. Still caught in that moment of timelessness in which nothing else in the world existed but them, they made love. It was a slow, deep, sustaining rhythm—a building ecstasy that would last a lifetime.

Later, as they lay side by side, Matt bent his head to

nuzzle her neck. "I realize this is a hell of a time and place to be discussing business," he began as his teeth sensuously grazed her earlobe, "but I might as well tell you now. I'm going to hire another pilot."

Mickie twisted around to look up into his laughing eyes. "I may love you, Matthew Greenslade, but I won't give up my forty percent," she replied with mock ferocity.

"That's another thing I wanted to talk to you about." His arm moved to circle her waist like a warm, strong band. "I think I've been a little too stubborn about this whole business." He was grinning openly by then. "I'm willing to make this partnership between Greenslade and Kilpatrick a fifty-fifty arrangement. . . . That's usually the way it is in a marriage, isn't it?"

"Is this a proposal, Matt?" she inquired gravely.

His eyes gleamed with loving laughter. "Do you want your business agent to look over the terms?" he teased. "Or do you think you can give me an answer here on the spot?"

Her eyes were still grave and questioning. "Do you love me, Matt?"

He dropped his bantering manner at once. "Forgive me for not saying it first. I've been waiting all my life for a woman like you, Mickie. I love and adore you."

"Matt," she whispered softly, not quite able to believe the flood of joy and fulfillment that surged within her as he took her in his powerful and tender embrace.

Hours later they sat wrapped in thick robes with mugs of Irish coffee on the hearth before them. Mickie's feet were curled up beneath her and her head lay against Matt's shoulders. The events of the previous days seemed like pages out of a half-forgotten past as she stared with bemused eyes into the flames. "Why did Sondra come to your room last night?"

"Because she thought she could make me forget about you."

Her previous denials of jealousy notwithstanding, Mickie's eyes clouded over for an instant. "Did she?"

Matt's warm laughter washed over her. "No chance, love. All I did was talk about you and what a hellion you were, how you'd tangled up my life until I couldn't think straight. Being a woman, she recognized the classic symptoms of a man who'd fallen hard but refused to admit it."

Mickie smiled mischievously. "You were just afraid to admit you'd finally met your match."

"You're hell on a man's ego," Matt retorted as he bent his head and nipped her earlobe lightly in punishment. "I couldn't believe it when I came up against your fiery strength of will. I'd never met a woman like you before."

"Yet you despised me for it," Mickie couldn't help putting in.

His expression became wry. "I thought I did. But then I realized that I was never bored when I was around you. You were one surprise after another."

"Are you sure you know what you're getting into?" she asked, laughing.

"Probably not," he retorted teasingly. "I'll never be quite sure what you're planning next." His eyes shone like golden flames. "You *are* planning a wedding, aren't you?"

"Of course I am. But Annie will insist that we can't get married until she's sewn me a full trousseau."

"Forget it," he growled. "The only trousseau you'll need is that flimsy white gown you wore on Russian Harbor. In fact, I think we'll rent the Revaks's bungalow for our honeymoon. You have a few more lessons coming."

He pulled her close once more and his mouth enveloped hers in a seductive foretaste of more to come.

When they drew apart at last Mickie asked him, "Matt, will we fly to Nevada so you can introduce me to your father?"

"Of course," he teased. "You don't think I'm going to tie you up in the bed furs and keep you helplessly captive to my advances for the rest of your life, do you?"

"I hope so," she replied, a breath of excitement passing through her as his hand reached out to lightly caress her bared shoulder.

"Good. That's why we'll need that third pilot," he teased again.

"But do you think your father will like me?" she asked, the question troubling her.

"He'll take one look at you, Mickie, with your red hair and stormy gray eyes, and then he'll turn to me. 'Matt,' he'll say, 'you'll never tame her.'"

Mickie smiled at her lover. "And what will you reply?"

Matt's eyes flashed beneath the thick black fringe of his lashes. "I'll tell him the truth: I don't even want to try."

Mickie leaned over him playfully and caught his lower lip between her teeth, nipping it sensually. "I'm your hellcat, Matt," she murmured against his mouth. "Your hellcat with wings."

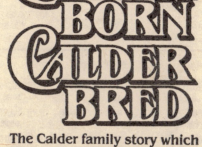

YOU'LL BE SWEPT AWAY WITH SILHOUETTE DESIRE

$1.75 each

1 ☐ CORPORATE AFFAIR
James

2 ☐ LOVE'S SILVER WEB
Monet

3 ☐ WISE FOLLY
Clay

4 ☐ KISS AND TELL
Carey

5 ☐ WHEN LAST WE
LOVED
Baker

6 ☐ A FRENCHMAN'S KISS
Mallory

7 ☐ NOT EVEN FOR LOVE
St. Claire

8 ☐ MAKE NO PROMISES
Dee

9 ☐ MOMENT IN TIME
Simms

10 ☐ WHENEVER I LOVE
YOU Smith

$1.95 each

11 ☐ VELVET TOUCH
James

12 ☐ THE COWBOY AND
THE LADY Palmer

13 ☐ COME BACK, MY
LOVE Wallace

14 ☐ BLANKET OF STARS
Valley

15 ☐ SWEET BONDAGE
Vernon

16 ☐ DREAM COME TRUE
Major

17 ☐ OF PASSION BORN
Simms

18 ☐ SECOND HARVEST
Ross

19 ☐ LOVER IN PURSUIT
James

20 ☐ KING OF DIAMONDS
Allison

21 ☐ LOVE IN THE CHINA
SEA Baker

22 ☐ BITTERSWEET IN
BERN Durant

23 ☐ CONSTANT
STRANGER Sunshine

24 ☐ SHARED MOMENTS
Baxter

25 ☐ RENAISSANCE MAN
James

26 ☐ SEPTEMBER
MORNING Palmer

27 ☐ ON WINGS OF NIGHT
Conrad

28 ☐ PASSIONATE
JOURNEY Lovan

29 ☐ ENCHANTED DESERT
Michelle

30 ☐ PAST FORGETTING
Lind

31 ☐ RECKLESS PASSION
James

32 ☐ YESTERDAY'S
DREAMS Clay

33 ☐ PROMISE ME
TOMORROW Powers

34 ☐ SNOW SPIRIT
Milan

35 ☐ MEANT TO BE
Major

36 ☐ FIRES OF MEMORY
Summers

37 ☐ PRICE OF SURRENDER
James

38 ☐ SWEET SERENITY
Douglass

39 ☐ SHADOW OF
BETRAYAL Monet

40 ☐ GENTLE CONQUEST
Mallory

41 ☐ SEDUCTION BY
DESIGN St. Claire

42 ☐ ASK ME NO SECRETS
Stewart

43 ☐ A WILD, SWEET
MAGIC Simms

44 ☐ HEART OVER MIND
West

45 ☐ EXPERIMENT IN LOVE
Clay

46 ☐ HER GOLDEN EYES
Chance

47 ☐ SILVER PROMISES
Michelle

48 ☐ DREAM OF THE WEST
Powers

49 ☐ AFFAIR OF HONOR
James

Silhouette Desire

50 ☐ FRIENDS AND LOVERS Palmer

51 ☐ SHADOW OF THE MOUNTAIN Lind

52 ☐ EMBERS OF THE SUN Morgan

53 ☐ WINTER LADY Joyce

54 ☐ IF EVER YOU NEED ME Fulford

55 ☐ TO TAME THE HUNTER James

56 ☐ FLIP SIDE OF YESTERDAY Douglass

57 ☐ NO PLACE FOR A WOMAN Michelle

58 ☐ ONE NIGHT'S DECEPTION Mallory

59 ☐ TIME STANDS STILL Powers

60 ☐ BETWEEN THE LINES Dennis

61 ☐ ALL THE NIGHT LONG Simms

62 ☐ PASSIONATE SILENCE Monet

63 ☐ SHARE YOUR TOMORROWS Dee

64 ☐ SONATINA Milan

65 ☐ RECKLESS VENTURE Allison

66 ☐ THE FIERCE GENTLENESS Langtry

67 ☐ GAMEMASTER James

68 ☐ SHADOW OF YESTERDAY Browning

69 ☐ PASSION'S PORTRAIT Carey

70 ☐ DINNER FOR TWO Victor

71 ☐ MAN OF THE HOUSE Joyce

72 ☐ NOBODY'S BABY Hart

73 ☐ A KISS REMEMBERED St. Claire

74 ☐ BEYOND FANTASY Douglass

75 ☐ CHASE THE CLOUDS McKenna

76 ☐ STORMY SERENADE Michelle

77 ☐ SUMMER THUNDER Lowell

78 ☐ BLUEPRINT FOR RAPTURE Barber

79 ☐ SO SWEET A MADNESS Simms

80 ☐ FIRE AND ICE Palmer

81 ☐ OPENING BID Kennedy

82 ☐ SUMMER SONG Clay

83 ☐ HOME AT LAST Chance

84 ☐ IN A MOMENT'S TIME Powers

85 ☐ THE SILVER SNARE James

86 ☐ NATIVE SEASON Malek

87 ☐ RECIPE FOR LOVE Michelle

88 ☐ WINGED VICTORY Trevor

89 ☐ TIME FOR TOMORROW Ross

90 ☐ WILD FLIGHT Roszel

SILHOUETTE DESIRE, Department SD/6
1230 Avenue of the Americas
New York, NY 10020

Please send me the books I have checked above. I am enclosing $_____
(please add 50¢ to the cover postage and handling. NYS and NYC residents please add appropriate sales tax.) Send check or money order—no cash or C.O.D.'s please. Allow six weeks for delivery.

NAME _____

ADDRESS _____

CITY _____ STATE/ZIP _____